by Conrad Richter

These are BORZOI BOOKS, *published in New York by* ALFRED A. KNOPF

The Grandfathers

The Grandfathers

CONRAD RICHTER

New York
ALFRED · A · KNOPF
1964

L. C. catalog card number: 64–13445

THIS IS A BORZOI BOOK,
PUBLISHED BY ALFRED A. KNOPF, INC.

Manufactured in the United States of America, and distributed by Random House, Inc.
Published simultaneously in Toronto, Canada, by Random House of Canada, Limited.

FIRST EDITION

ACKNOWLEDGMENTS

I WANT to thank Sarah Culbert, John Brommer, Lloyd Alderman, Dr. John J. B. Light, John Jones, the Rev. Thaxton Springfield, John G. Callender, J. Hampton Haldeman, John A. Schlappich, Caleb S. Christ, Slater Yocum, Irvin J. Leffler, Stanley L. and Emma R. Achenbach, Elvin and Grace and others of Maryland, West Virginia, and Pennsylvania who generously furnished material and suggestions.

The Grandfathers

CHAPTER I

I T was early morning in Western Maryland and already the whole Murdoch clan had been in to see the twins. That is, all except Granpap. He wouldn't come down from his shanty along the run. He acted mad every time a new baby turned up, let alone two. The babies couldn't help it, Chariter thought. The rest of the family had wasted no time to have a look at them. Chariter's mam and granmam had been in the shed room with Ant Dib all night. Chariter herself was next to see them. Uncle Heb had come in about daylight, stuffing his shirt into his pants. He slept in his heavy underclothes summer and winter. Now he jiggled a huge finger in each tiny fist. Uncle Nun came after, still barefoot, smiling his strong white teeth in his brown beard.

"Dib's the smart one, getting them wholesale," he said. "Now if I just knew how to get two days' pay for one lick of work."

Uncle Nun's jokes were famous in the family. He could say anything, and they'd laugh. Today on the strength of the occasion, he gave two or three.

"You're lucky they's a boy and girl so you know which one to keep." He turned to Chariter since Dib paid attention only to her babes. "Not like Uncle Robby told me once. He had a foxhound bitch gave him two pups exactly alike. Both dogs, same markings, same pap and mam. He couldn't make up his mind which one to keep. He took them out on the mountain and tried to lose the poor one, but they both came home. He took 'em to town to see which would stick by him. They both laid outside the barroom door till he come out about two or three in the morning. 'I tell you what,' Uncle Robby said, 'when you get two alike, it's mighty hard to tell which one to get rid of.' "

Now, Uncle Nun said, he'd have to eat or he wouldn't get any laggin' for the day. He and Uncle Heb were splitting dead chestnut stubs over in Jeffs Valley. Soon after he went Chariter's half-brother, Babe, came in rubbing his eyes with one hand and carrying Honour, whom they called Honey, with the other. After him came his older half-brother, Wellington, known as Fox. Both blinked at the twins.

"Chariter, do you want to go up and tell Mrs. Stevens your Ant Dib can't come today?" Granmam said. It was more of an order than a question. "You kin tell her your mam'll come if she wants her."

"You didn't ask me!" Dockey called out.

Granmam paid her no attention. She ruled the roost. "Now, Chariter, you do like I say."

The girl stood there contemplating. She was fifteen, able bodied and strong minded as her mother but not so quick to go on her muscle. Her mother was heavy and "yaller" haired. Ant Dib was skinny and dark-complected. Dockey said she had horse hair. Granpap claimed it was the Indian in her from Granmam. Chariter took after neither, being red headed with red-brown eyes. She heard Nobe Gandy once say, "You'd never guess she came out of them Murdochs." That had been when she was little and she'd wondered for a long time how she was different. Now she stood thinking how her mam or granmam, if they wanted, could have gone across the fields and phoned Mrs. Stevens from the Magills, but never would they. No, they didn't like a contraption of wires and wall box any more than they did a flush toilet, preferring the woods. Well, she guessed, she did, too. She'd never worked a flush toilet yet. Mam said every time she set one off up at the Stevenses she thought the blamed thing was going to choke up and spill out everything on the floor, and what a mess she would have to clean up then.

When Chariter went out, the young ones trailed along, Babe toting Honey.

"Mrs. Stevens ain't never seen her yet," he begged.

"And she ain't liable to see her now," Chariter said. "A lady don't have her eyes open yet this time of day. You can take her along if you want to, but it's too far and she's too heavy for you. Fox, you take her."

Fox grumbled. When they got to the Stevens's mail box, they all stopped to admire the red bird painted on it.

"How come they have such a thumping big mail bin?" Babe wanted to know.

"Rich folks get letters all the way from Baltimore," Fox told him. "I heerd they got a mighty big post office in Baltimore."

At the crick Fox got Chariter to carry Honey. He wanted to expound to Babe all the Murdochs had done for the Stevenses. If it hadn't been for Uncle Heb and Uncle Nun, he said, they wouldn't have a place to live in. It was them who had cut and dragged the timber for this here bridge and planted all these pine whips, though Uncle Heb said he threw most of his in the crick when nobody was looking. The big white mansion house on the other side of the meadow they helped build out of the old Kitteredge farm house. They roofed and painted the barn, too, though it held nary cow, horse nor chicken, and they bedrocked this here red shell lane for the Stevens automobile to roll over.

Not that Fox and the other were on it. They had taken the shortcut across the bottom pasture to the barn.

"Now you young ones stay here under the forbey," Chariter told them. "And mind you, don't go inside or if it burns down the sheriff'll blame you like he did Granpap for Dusenberry's." She handed Honey back to Fox and started across the fine mowed lawn for the house.

Going over she remembered the first time she had been sent here with news like this. That was when her mother had Honey. The Stevenses were new to the valley then and Mam hadn't worked there long. The girl had knocked three times, first light, then harder and at last loud enough to wake the dead. After while a sleepy looking lady in a pink throw had come to the door.

"Mam can't come today," Chariter told her. "She had her baby last night."

Mrs. Stevens's blue eyes had widened.

"Her baby! You mean born to her? Why I never— she said nothing about it to me."

"No, you could hardly tell it on her," Chariter agreed soberly. "She carried it low."

"I didn't even know Dockey was married," Mrs. Stevens said.

7

The girl had just looked away and waited till she thought the lady had got hold of herself. The Murdochs liked no funny business over this thing. But you could see Mrs. Stevens wasn't satisfied.

"I remember Dockey mentioned other children from time to time. Are they all at your house?"

"There's three," the girl said without expression.

"You must tell me their names so I know all of you," Mrs. Stevens had smiled brightly. "You can begin with yourself."

"I'm Chariter."

"And your cousins?"

"I got none I know of," the girl told her. "Just Fox and Babe."

Mrs. Stevens had repeated the names doubtfully.

"These are boys or girls?"

"They're my brothers."

"And their last names?"

"It's Murdoch, like me."

She could see that underneath Mrs. Stevens was mightily puzzled. Outside she had brightened.

"Now you must tell me their mothers' names."

"They're all mam's," the girl said, watching her closely. She had decided it was the extent of what she was going to say.

All this came back to her mind now, for it hadn't happened so long ago. But today when the lady came to the door, she took the news about Ant Dib without fuss or feathers.

"Isn't that nice, Chariter," she said when she heard there were twins. "And a boy and a girl! Have you names for them yet? How is your Aunt Dib feeling?"

The girl told her she guessed Ant Dib felt like always, anyhow far as she could tell. Then she remembered her mission.

"Granmam said Mam can come if you want her?"

"Indeed I do. Could she come this morning?"

"I'll tell her," Chariter promised, but she didn't go, waiting to be dismissed as was seemly for a Murdoch by a Stevens.

"Well, I'm grateful to you for coming over. Tell your Aunt Dib to show me the twins sometime. I'd love to see them." Mrs. Stevens smiled graciously and the girl knew it was her cue.

Going back to the barn she kept thinking about that smile. A medicine peddler had once told Granmam that her redhaired grandchild had such a nice smile. But hers was different than Mrs. Stevens's. She had to feel like it to turn it on. All the Murdochs were that way. They showed right off how they felt. They could be nice if they wanted, but holding back, scowling and yelling came just as easy, and that's what they did a lot of the time. Now it seemed like Mrs. Stevens could smile and act nice no matter how she felt. Chariter reckoned that was what made her a lady. She tried smiling without feeling like it on the way back to the barn.

"What are you grinning at?" Fox wanted to know, but Babe smiled back at her happily.

"I seen her!" he crowed. "I seen the lady come out on the porch in her wrapper."

"Mam calls it a bathrobe," Chariter said.

"I didn't see no bathrobe," Fox told her. "But I seen that wired-in porch upstairs. That's where Ant Dib says they sleep like chickens on a tree that won't come in the hen house at night."

"I guess they like fresh air, don't they Chariter?" Babe said. "Granpap likes fresh air for his feet. He says he can't sleep unless they're sticking out from the covers."

"It's not fresh air with him. It's contrariness," Chariter told him. "He sticks his feet out and his head under."

"I seen her but I didn't him," Babe complained. "Did you see him, Chariter? Mam says he only eats one egg for breakfast."

"I seen him more'n once," Fox boasted. "He's puny. You kin tell he's a one-egg man just by looking at him."

"I kin eat three myself," Babe said. "If Uncle Heb don't eat seven, he ain't feeling good."

"He ate nine once," Fox bragged. "And Uncle Nun thirteen."

"Granpap's puny but he's no one-egg man," Babe said. "Last night I heerd him bawling down to Uncle Heb to bring up a slice of hog cheek between bread. He done it too."

"Yes and he'd better or Granpap would a licked him," Fox declared.

As they started back, Chariter remembered the time Granpap had put in these young trees. Uncle Heb and Uncle Nun were over in Jeffs Valley when Mrs. Stevens had sent for them, so Granpap said he'd come. He needed a couple of dollars for liquor. Mrs. Stevens had wanted somebody to transplant young hemlocks from their mountain land to both sides of their lane. Granpap had showed up at her back door with a shovel, a grubbing hoe and a whole raft of young hemlocks he had pulled out, stolen, you might say, from the Magills' swamp where they couldn't see him. He had done it on the way over so he wouldn't have to "tromp" all over the couple hundred acres of Stevens mountain land looking for what would suit her.

"Where did you get such beautiful young trees?" Mrs. Stevens had asked him.

"Oh, right at home," Granpap had lied. "I don't like a hemlock around. It moans too much in the wind."

That night Mam had come home and told Granmam what Mrs. Stevens had said about Granpap, that she had expected a big fierce man from what she had heard. Instead she found him the nicest obliging little man. He hadn't even charged her for the hemlocks he had so generously brought from home. Chariter gave a little laugh. Mrs. Stevens ought to see Granpap on a rampage. Then maybe she wouldn't think him so meek and obliging.

CHAPTER II

THE Murdoch place lay on a white oak knoll. On one side ran the open upland fields of the Magills and on the other side far beyond the woods rolled the red-shell land of Wichita Leck. Down below the knoll nearer the road was the house where Tom Leck lived away from Wichita.

They were the only two houses you could see from the road right there, at least in the summer time, and once you went up the Murdoch lane in the woods you didn't see either one till you got up on the knoll to a half clearing with the weathered Murdoch house standing in the trees, its loft and shed rooms added piece by piece, and around it the pigpen, smokehouse, chicken pen, wagon shed, the stable they called the barn and a little old trolley without wheels that Granpap had got for nothing and hauled out on a wagon years ago. It was the only piece on the Murdoch place that had once been painted. Granpap used to sleep in it but of late it was too close to the house to suit him.

"Let me out of here!" he hollered one night when Dockey had men callers making a racket. Next day he had Nun and Heb help him start a shanty up on the fork where water from a sand spring joined the run coming out of the gap between the two benches on the mountain. Nobody lived back there, and summer and winter the Murdochs used the run for water. There was none better, Granpap said. He'd drunk out of a dozen mountains, but that from their own Black Log was the clearest and coldest. Black Log Mountain stood over the Murdochs mighty close, shading them late afternoons when the white oaks didn't. On a hot day towards suppertime the valley knew it had already started to get cool at the Murdochs.

Was it two or was it three weeks after the twins came that the family had another increase? Chariter rode home with Granmam from tending market in Dumont and found a stranger sprawled on the slab bench between two white oaks. Well, he wasn't altogether a stranger. She'd seen him around about nine or ten months ago but not lately. Once you laid eyes on a whale of a man like him you didn't forget him. He was that powerful, Uncle Nun said, they didn't have to back the team around anymore. This fellow could lift up the rear of the wagon and drag the wheels after. She didn't know his last name yet. They called him Chick.

"How are you, Mam? How are you, Chariter?" he called big and pleased as a bull with two tails. He lay there on his back, lifting nothing but his hand. Now what was he up to? Chariter wondered, calling Granmam, Mam, and saying her own name. He had never said beans to her before.

Supper came and the big man sat down with them at the table. That wasn't uncommon its own self. Most anybody who stuck around was asked to have a bite with them. But the way he joked at the table to Uncle Heb and Nun and even to Granpap was more than he had to. He was still around when she went to bed in the loft and when she got up next morning.

"What's he here for?" Fox demanded of Chariter who sat on the stool milking.

"Mam says he heard about the twins and come to get a look at them," she told him.

"A man like him!" Fox disbelieved.

"Mam says he's their pappy," she explained.

"Well, what if he is?" Fox said. "He's seen 'em now, why don't he go?"

Chariter couldn't answer that one. It had never happened around here before. They'd had a mam, ant, uncles, a granpappy and granmam, yes, but not more.

She'd keep her eyes open and her wits working. Maybe she could find out about this strange thing if he stayed long enough. She hadn't need to wonder about that. By the middle of next week it looked like this was home to Chick Saylor. He went out on the job with Uncles Nun and Heb over in Jeffs Valley. Uncle Heb said they didn't need a horse when Chick was around. He could drag a log down the skidway himself.

What took Chariter was the way a man like him carried on with those twins. Later on she wondered if something inside had told him his twins would never grow up, that less than a week before starting school, they would take spine fever, the boy first, the girl soon after, and both die within twenty four hours of each other. Not that you'd guess it today from the spunk and muscle they showed. Why, already the second week Jess could lift his head. That boy was going to be like his old daddy, Chick said.

Most every evening he toted them out to a stump, always the boy but sometimes both, rocking Jess sitting up in one arm and Jessie halfways up in the other, fetching out a tune in his funny high pitched voice for such a whale of a man. Those twins didn't seem more than rag dolls in his hands. Sundays if it didn't rain too hard he'd take Jess down to Stevens's grove, talking to him like a man talks to a dog or pollparrot, holding him out over the crick till his little naked feet splashed in the cold water, telling him that when he got older he was going to let him all the way down and then he had to swim or go to the bottom. Chariter told herself it looked like Chick was going to be around a long time.

Not that he and Ant Dib didn't have their squabbles. More than once she had it out hot and heavy with him, and one time she threw him out of their shed room bag and baggage. You wouldn't reckon a woman could do that to a powerful man like Chick but out he went and his things after.

"And don't you ever come back!" she yelled.

"I ain't a going any place," he said to Granpap who had come down from his shanty to watch sympathetically and listen. "No woman can run me off from my own flesh and blood. Some day that little feller might need his old daddy and when he does I figger to be around."

He slept up with Granpap that night. The next day he and Ant Dib were together again like nothing had happened, and Chariter looked with new eyes on Chick. He had given her a thing or two to think about. Not only her but Babe.

"How do you reckon the twins like having Chick for a pappy?" he asked plaintively.

"I guess they like it," she said. "They act that way."

"How does Chick know he's pappy to them?" Babe went on.

"If Chick says he's pappy to them, I reckon he is," Chariter said. "And Dib never said he wasn't."

"I asked Mam one time who daddied me and she said I didn't have none," Babe persisted. "She said she found me out behind a stump."

"What stump was that?" Fox jeered. "The one with a groundhog hole under it? Maybe your pap was a groundhog."

"Now I heard enough about this," Chariter told him.

"Maybe it's good Mam didn't tell him," Fox went on plaguing. "Maybe his pap got hung."

Babe winced, looking anxiously at his half sister.

"You don't say that, do you, Chariter?"

"No, I don't. And Fox don't know any more about it than you do," she told him.

"I wouldn't like him getting in trouble with the sheriff," Babe said.

"Maybe if you get in trouble with the sheriff some day, you'll find out who your pap is," Chariter consoled him. "He might come forward and bail you out."

"I don't want to know where I come from," Fox announced. "Maybe he kain't talk, only mumbles like Tom Leck's brother. Maybe he's a half wit. You ought to be able to pick the pap you want. You don't have to keep a horse or dog if you don't want to."

Chariter looked at him compassionately. She made no comment on his revelation. She had had thoughts like that herself.

"Don't you know where I come from, Chariter?" Babe persisted.

"You come from right here," she said vigorously. "And it's a good enough place to come from."

"Didn't no man even come around to hist me up when I was little?"

"I disremember," she put him off.

"Why do you reckon Chick come around and my pap didn't?"

"I don't know except I heard Mam say once she didn't want any man laying around the house to have to look at every day. She didn't want to be like Granmam putting up with Granpap day in and day out and nights too. I reckon that's the way it was with Wichita and Tom and why they put all that ground betweeen them. They couldn't stand seeing each other around."

"Ant Dib stands seeing Chick around."

The girl didn't say anything.

"Doesn't she, Chariter?" Babe kept on.

"Now that's enough, Babe," she turned on him. "Just see that no woman can't stand seeing you around."

"You kin stand seeing me around, kain't you, Chariter?"

"Sometimes," she said vigorously. "Maybe I couldn't

if you was growed. Folks feel nicer towards young ones. You get mean and ugly when you grow up. If young boys was ugly and ornery as Granpap, their mams would never raise them."

"Didn't Mam ever tell you who daddied you?"

"No," Chariter said shortly. "She told me she didn't know."

"How come she don't when Ant Dib does?" Babe stuck to it.

"I can't tell you," Chariter scolded him. "But I can tell you one thing. I'm getting mighty tired of hearing about your pappy this and your pappy that. I'll tell you now whoever he is he ain't much or he'd a come around to lay eyes on you when you was little taking your first toddle. And that goes for mine, too. We're in the same boat. If he can forget you that easy, you better do the same with him."

"Don't you ever reckon sometimes what yours looks like?" Babe ventured.

"I don't ever give him a face," Chariter told him bleakly. "I just hide him behind a bush in my mind."

That's what she thought she did and had done it, too. But now since Chick had come in the family she found it a harder chore. On the slow drive to market in the early blackness with Granmam she found herself going over the places in the valley they passed and the same coming back in the midday sunlight. Her mind wool gathered, set off by the galvanized iron mail boxes standing on one leg at every house or lane, the sad ones leaning or sagging, the righteous ones standing up straight. None save the Stevens and Goddem boxes had a name painted on it, not even a number. Felty, the rural mail carrier, knew them all, and if he didn't, his old horse did. Chariter knew them, too, and what's more, the faces that came or used to come to open those boxes after Felty had passed. Some of those faces now for all her boast to Babe started to hang in her mind.

Riding home in broad daylight she seldom had the sand to talk about it, and going down in the dark she felt too sleepy. But one day with the rain pelting down on the top of the spring wagon and certain faces sticking in her mind, she ventured.

"Will you tell me something if I ask you, Granmam?" she asked.

"I will if I kin," her granmam answered.

"Did you know of anything between Mam and some man in the valley one time?"

"Yes, and between your mam and some other men," her granmam said promptly.

"I know that," Chariter said. "I mean before I came along."

"That's what I mean," Granmam declared.

The girl thought that over.

"Do you mind yet who they were, Granmam?"

"Oh, I mind clear as last night, but I don't know as I want to say."

"Why don't you?"

"You kin ask your mam your own self," Granmam told her shortly.

The girl waited a day to corner her mother coming in from the barn. Her mam stood forbidding in the path.

"I tole you once," she said. "You asked me that before."

"No, you didn't tell me," Chariter stood her ground. "Anyway, I'm asking you again."

"You ask me for a lie and I'll tell you one."

"I don't want any lie," Chariter said.

"Then you kin take your ruthers," her mother told her and went past.

So she had her ruthers, Chariter told herself, whatever that meant. Well, that's what she got for speaking out on her mam's business. And now she didn't know any more than she did before. But that didn't mean it had to stay that way.

CHAPTER III

THE oak grove around the Murdochs was a place for loafing. Warm Sundays certain men, if you asked them, would say they weren't going much of any place, but if you followed, you'd find they ended up around Granpap's old trolley. Hardly a Sunday in mild weather that you couldn't hear disputes out there. Generally they lay between Tom Leck and Nobe Gandy. What those two wrangled over most times was a poser to Chariter. She had the feeling they talked in riddles, that something lay under their strange arguments. Now why did those two old men lock horns so much?

"When Sip Leck and Morg Gandy were in school did they fight all the time like their paps?" she asked Uncle Nun once.

Uncle Nun had only laughed.

Now why did he laugh? Chariter pondered, and had it anything to do with the way those two old men acted toward her? Their women, too. They treated her different than they did Babe or Fox, or Ant Dib and Granmam either.

She couldn't help but notice it today with Fulliam along. He had showed up for his day off early this morning. He said it was the only time the last two weeks they didn't have a body on the cooling board. He and Chariter had started going with each other in valley school. Granpap called him wild as a whaup and touchy as tinder. Not so, Chariter said. Never would she want to mate up with anybody wild as Granpap. Granmam had done that and regretted it. Fulliam just couldn't sit still long as other folks. He had too much sap. Besides, he was older than she was and that's why he quit school last year and started in as an undertaker's helper for his namesake uncle in Earlville.

"That'll tame him," Granpap said at the time. "All them bodies will sober him down."

But Chariter couldn't see much difference when he came home to the valley some week ends. You still had to handle him right. Uncle Nun said it was lucky corpses weren't hot blooded or he'd dispute with them. Today Fulliam was docile enough, glad to get Chariter away from the house even if he did have to go along to the neighbors for eggs for Granmam to take to market.

The Lecks was the first place they went to. You really couldn't call it the Lecks' place but Wichita's.

They saw old Tom in his blacksmith shop across the crick shrinking a tire on a felloe as they passed. He was the one who gave Chariter her child's ring years ago, claiming he found it in the soft coal for his forge. How a brand new silver ring with a tiny red stone could get in coal from the mines, Tom didn't say. Chariter wondered about that ring today as they went up the lane past the spot where Tom and Wichita's boy, Sip, had got stuck in the mud last March. It was the first time he came out in his brand new machine and he had to be pulled out by Russel Allyn who did a little farming for Wichita.

Oh, Sip was mostly what Wichita talked about. His full name was Cyprus, pronounced Siprus in the valley. She was always saying Siprus this and Siprus that to Chariter, telling her the good ways he had and how they came from her side of the house. The woman was a talker and no mistake. Tom claimed she weighed three hundred pounds but never could he get her on a scale. Once he had made out with Purcell at the coal yard to weigh them both in the road wagon. He had weighed himself alone in it the week before. But Wichita had jumped out screaming at the weighmaster before he could set the weights.

Her's was one place where Chariter would rather not have had Fulliam along. She had to do too many chores for Wichita when she came, gather the eggs, draw water for Star and carry some out to the field crocks for her white Leghorns. Then like as not she'd be asked to milk Star though it might be only the middle of the afternoon. Today Wichita said she'd keep Fulliam company if Chariter would pull some rhubarb for her granmam to take along to market for her and maybe the girl could find where one of her geese had stolen its nest.

"I'm glad I have Chariter. I can't get around like I used to," she told Fulliam who said nothing. Oh, you could see there was little he missed but all he said on the way out was that Wichita Leck would take an oversize coffin and that would run into extra money.

After Wichita's, they crossed the valley to the Gandys. Their place was high up on a long cleared bench of Kettle Mountain. Nobe had never given Chariter anything save chestnuts he'd picked from young trees not yet blighted, but Effie, his mite of a woman, had deviled her one time about a dress. Wouldn't Chariter like a new one? she had put to her with the brightest black eyes. She had even showed her the goods for it, white with green vines and roses printed on it. Oh, it was handsome, the girl thought. Effie said she had the best part of a bolt of it, eight yards anyway, and it wouldn't take more than five or six. Chariter was hardly twelve then. Effie said she had the goods folded up for fifteen or twenty years in her bureau drawer, just as good as the day she bought it.

Better, in fact, for they didn't make dress goods that good any more. The girl had dreampt about that new dress for a year.

Today when she and Fulliam got up the rutty lane with her baskets, Vedna left them in. She was Morg's sister living over in West Virginia. Chariter and Fulliam had to sit down and have a piece of Meadow Mountain cake while Effie and Vedna told them how Morg had moved back from Memphis. Vedna took a snapshot of him from her pocketbook and showed it to the girl, watching all the time with sharp eyes and the queerest set to her face while Chariter looked at the picture. It meant nothing to the girl, just a strange man older looking than she expected, with a bald head, a hairy mustache and a fiddle in his hand. She handed it to Fulliam and when she didn't say anything, Vedna looked at her mother disappointed.

When they left, Nobe stopped her under the big maple tree.

"Ain't it pretty here, Chariter?" he exulted. He looked around at the hog pen, the broken netting of the chicken pen, the barn with its roof sagging and the corncrib down to the last cob. All were unpainted and weather beaten. "No, but ain't it pretty here? There's no nicer spot in the valley. You're up high enough to catch a breeze and see who's on the road. Of course, it has a few things around here I might do if I wanted, but

I can't go it night and day like I used to. No, but ain't it a nice place up here?"

What was he getting at, Chariter wondered, for Vince Foote said he had gone hunting on the mountain with Nobe last fall and Nobe had worn him plumb out.

"And them Prideleys trying to take it away from me!" Nobe suddenly began to shout. "All they done was lend me a little money to pay a note. I didn't want to insult them reading the paper they gave me to sign. When I heerd what was in that paper I went up to them. 'Ed,' I said, 'I hear you bought our place for a song?' 'Yep,' he said. 'I guess it's my place now.' Wasn't that some way to talk?" Nobe started yelling louder. "Why, my pap was born right up in that room under the eaves and his pap before him. But Ed guessed wrong. I took it to court and the jury gave me a paper. You know what it said?"

There was no use Chariter saying she'd heard it before. He'd recite it anyway. He went on triumphantly.

"It said this place could be had by me and my survivors as long as they lived." He gave Chariter a playful push on the shoulder. "That's a pretty long time, ain't it? Twelve men good and true signed that paper. It says I kin stay here as long as I live, and my survivors after me."

His eyes misted at her in unexplained emotion.

"That means you, Chariter. Vedna and her man

have a place of their own in West Virginia, and now Morg's got a house across the river. They don't need this place when we're gone. Them twelve men good and true might as well a set down your name."

Chariter was puzzled by those words. Could it mean what he said? she asked herself, for not every girl of fifteen is promised a house and farm. Whatever it meant, she'd say nothing at home. Most likely it didn't mean any more than the dress. She had never got that and she'd never get this either.

Going down to the road she felt uneasy over what the Gandys had said in front of Fulliam. But she needn't have. All Fulliam acted like he knew was the undertaking and the furniture business. It gave her a good feeling. That was one thing he did, carry out his end of the unspoken bargain between them. Never did he let on he knew about her father and she the same about his mother. Of the two, the girl guessed, what his mam did was the worse. Chariter used to see her at market where she had a stall the year round, driving down in her spring wagon twice a week with eggs, home baked bread, pies and rolls, green truck and berries in season, bunches of flowers in summer, red oak and gum leaves in the fall and crowfoot and pine in winter. In time she paid off the farm. She told Granmam at market it was clear now and she could rest easy in bed at night. The load was off her back. She'd carried it a long while, for

Fulliam's pap hardly broke even on the farm. But he had big ideas like Fulliam. One day she came from market and found he had the cement contractor from Dumont getting ready to start a concrete silo, lay cement floors in the horse and cow stable so he could keep them clean, and a cement walk from the house to the barn. He said he was tired of tramping in the mire when it rained. Till he got through it had set them back in debt seventeen hundred dollars. One cold morning that winter they found her hanging in the cow stable over the cement floor that was dirty now as it had ever been before. Folks at the funeral told Asa it was too bad his wife had got melancholy, but all knew it was the concrete in the barn.

After supper Fulliam said he had to get back to Earlville. Chariter walked him down the lane. When he left she saw her mam coming down the road and they went up the lane together, unspeaking until they could see the house.

"Now you be keerful with that feller," Dockey told her harshly.

"You're a good one to tell me," Chariter said in a low voice.

"I'll tell you what I please," Dockey flared.

"Well, don't you say nothing bad about him," the girl warned. "He's good enough for me."

"They're all good and bad," her mam said. "The

trouble is they're more bad than good and I'll tell you to be keerful with any one of them."

"I can take care of myself," Chariter said.

"Well, see then that you do," her mother told her.

CHAPTER IV

SUNDAY morning came to Kettle Valley mild and clear after early fog. By nine o'clock they were gathering under the white oaks, Tom Leck, Nobe Gandy and Vince Foote, who lived with his sister up the valley. The fresh young baby leaves of the oaks had just started to push, making the out-of-doors look soft and new. You'd guess the whole world pure and innocent as a newborn babe if you didn't know any different.

Chariter lay on one of the old weathered slabs nailed between two trees, looking up at the dangle of pink and green overhead. She wanted to hear some of that strange talk between Tom and Nobe today. Always had it sounded curious, like some secret business those two knew but she didn't. Generally about the time their talk started to give her notions, Granmam or Ant Dib would send her off on some chore, almost on purpose, it looked like. Today she made up her mind she'd stick around.

Maybe what they said wasn't the riddle she once thought. All she had to do was wait till Tom cut her mam's corns and calluses.

He sat on a stump with his patient tilted back in the old handmade willow chair they kept out in the weather.

"Now you go easy!" Dockey complained, scruching around and getting hold of the chair arms.

She's snorting, Tom," Nun said. "She's showing the whites of her eyes. I'd rope up her leg like you done to Jim Miller's mare."

"Hell, I hardly touched her yet," the blacksmith told him, trimming up the first callus with the expert pride of a masterhand at shaving off the horny stuff of horses' and man's extremities. But he hadn't gone far till Dockey gave out a yell.

"Watch out, Tom Leck, what you're doing!"

"You stabbed her in the quick of the hoof that time," Nobe said.

"I wasn't even near it," the blacksmith complained. "Unless it could be a stone blister. I found one once in the frog on Dusenberry's sorrel. When I opened it up, the matter squirted out black as coal. But you don't need to fret, Dockey. I put that hoof in a bag with a poultice of cow dung and it was all right in a month."

"Shut up, you and your cow dung!" Dockey told him.

33

"Now if it was up at your joint it might be traveling gravel," the blacksmith plagued her. "You know Ray Harger's old grey. Her hoof took in a pointy stone. Six months later it come out the joint. She was lame all that time."

"Well, I ain't lame and don't have nothing wrong with my joint," Dockey told him.

Tom whetted the razor on his boot and gradually Dockey settled back. All was fairly quiet till he got to the corns. Then he pulled out his specs and sized up gravely what he had to do.

"No wonder you stabbed me," Dockey called out. "Why didn't you put on them things long ago?"

Chariter turned her back. She had heard all this several times before. She lay there while her mam abused Tom for butchering her.

"You better grab dirt and hold her tongue," Granpap advised. "If it was me, I'd put a twitch on her nose and throw her in the stocks!"

"The best pacifier for a nervous mare," Vince Foote put in, "is a drunk to hold her."

"Or a half wit," Nun said. "You mind, Tom, the time Al Fuller brung in that bay that was hell to shoe?"

"I mind," Tom growled. "He had me to the wall squeezing the guts out of me. Al had to take the sledge hammer to him to get me out. I told him he could take him to somebody else to shoe. I wouldn't touch him.

Then that simple McGaffey boy that died come in the shop. He hadn't enough sense to be scared. He took hold of that tail and said, 'Blaver, kaver, daver, ovvy, dovey, puvvy.' You know how he talked. You didn't know a thing he said, but the horse knowed he wasn't right in his mind. The minute the boy touched him he put his head down. A minute before his eyes were like saucers at me. Now he let me get under him and put four shoes on him like he was some old broken down hack."

"You don't need a half wit to hold my tail," Dockey said sharply. "Just go easy and don't cut off my toe with that thing."

"Barnaby Hill had a corn plagued him so bad he had Uncle Robby take off the toe with a cold chisel," Granpap put in. 'Now don't you throw that toe away,' Uncle Robby told him. 'Stick it in the ground somewheres handy to where you get buried. Then you won't lack nothing when you're gathered at the river.' "

Chariter lay there gapping. It sounded like all they were going to do today was bicker over cutting corns. She got up and moved off. Twice she came back to make sure she hadn't missed anything. Once Tom was talking about the side weights he'd put on her mother if she was a pacer instead of a work horse and next time Uncle Nun was recollecting the Browns Valley man who never changed his socks till he threw them up and they stuck fast to the ceiling. It looked like there'd be

35

no disputes between Nobe and Tom today. That's the way life went. Go fishing and the fish wouldn't bite. Sit Sundays on the Stevens's bridge and they jumped all around you. Well, she had enough riddle without Nobe and Tom making more. The world was a riddle, her mam, too, and the biggest of all was her own self. Some folks you could spell out easy like Ant Dib's eight day clock that ticked and struck all over the place. Other folks were like the seven jewel watch Uncle Nun had got at Sears Roebuck. The wheels went so quiet you couldn't hear them unless you put it to your head.

The third time she came back she pricked up her ears. Her mam was gone and Nobe talking. It sounded like riddle talk to her.

"I read in the paper the other day how some doctor grafted a live rabbit's eye on a blind man to see. Now how do they expect that man to go to sleep at night? A rabbit stays awake at night. Isn't that what they call nocturnal?"

"I wasn't talking about a rabbit's eye," Tom came back at him. "I was talking about a human. Eyes is the same as hair. They got to get their color from somebody back in the family line."

The girl listened closely. Nobe argued back.

"Not everybody with red hair in his blood has it come out on him. Take Max Waley in Tinsburg. His hair was black as a tinker's pot and his woman's the same. Their young one's hair come out red like their next door neighbor. Folks snickered so Max raised a mustache to show them. It come out red like Morg's mustache."

"Well, my sister Sal don't need to raise a mustache to show the red hair in our family," Tom told him. "She had red hair when she was little and still had it the last time I seen her."

"I seen her," Nobe scorned. "That's a different kind of red. That kind goes with a terrible temper."

"I know somebody," Tom said, "who got yaller hair and a terrible temper."

"You kin let Dockey out of this, Tom," Granmam broke in. "Chariter, what are you standing around for? You go in and peel some potatoes for dinner."

The girl never moved.

"It has other things that come down besides hair," Nobe was saying. "One of them things stands up in any court in the land."

"What's that?" Tom asked suspiciously.

Nobe put out a hand.

"Our school reader called it the universal language."

"You mean cursing?" Granpap wondered.

Nobe gave a look of disgust.

"I'm talking about the speech of angels. Some families

have it running in the blood and some don't. If you don't, you don't."

"Well, say what it is!" Granpap barked at him.

"Music," Nobe said.

"Sip had a drum when he was little," Tom told him. "Wichita got it for him in Dumont. He kept time with the damned thing like he was in the band."

"A drum!" Nobe said with great contempt. "That's noise, not music. Could he play the organ or mouth organ? Well, Morg could."

"Music runs in the Murdochs," Granpap asserted.

"The Murdochs! Which one of you could ever keep a tune besides Chariter?"

"Nun kin," Heb said. "I hear him singing once in a while out on the track. Show 'em, Nun."

Nun looked pleased and a little embarrassed.

"I got to have an axe for it," he tried to get out of it, but Heb fetched the axe for him. Nun went to a white oak and started taking swings at it, at first silently then fetching out a sing-song, the "huf" unspoken, coming out with a rush of breath at each clip.

Hi don diddy and I hit him in the eye. Huf!
Hi don diddy and I hit him on the nose. Huf!
Hi don diddy and I hit him in the eye. Huf!
Hi don diddy and I hit him in the nose. Huf.
He stopped and looked around.

"It has a lot of verses like that. I heerd Abe Coutts sing it one time. I never ast him the name."

"Name!" Nobe exploded. "Such carryings on don't have a name any more than a bullfrog croaking. I mean real tunes like Morg could play before he even went to school. He sang words to 'em, too. It used to make the eye water."

"If it come out of Morg's eye, it must of been stronger than water," Tom said.

Nobe looked sad.

"He don't go for that any more. He hasn't touched a drop since he's married."

"Did he or his woman tell you?"

Nobe held himself back.

"He's got religion. Holds gospel meetings Saturdays and Sundays. Plays the fiddle and him and his woman preach and save souls."

"She better save his first," Tom told him.

"You know what it says in the Bible," Nobe said bitterly. "A prophet don't have no honor in his own country. Well, you kin hear him preach for yourselves, if you're not shamed to show your face in meeting. He's coming to the school house. Two weeks from today."

"You better hide your hard cider when he comes," Tom jeered.

Granpappy suddenly came to life. He jumped up and scratched his back violently against a tree.

"Git me something to eat!" he bellowed to Heb. "And no apple butter bread, mind you. Fetch me some cold hog meat and horse radish."

"You don't do nothing of the kind," Granmam told Heb. "He kin wait for his dinner like the rest of us."

She got up and started for the house. Chariter went along, unseen objects rising in her mind like fish to the top of the crick for air. She wondered if she didn't know something about this business now. Even her Granpap Murdoch, she recollected, used to give his grandchildren a small fancy once in a while.

CHAPTER V

I T TOOK a long time for Chariter to get her rest this
Saturday night. Most times she couldn't count ten before dropping off. Tonight she kept turning this way
and that like a hex lay in bed with her. The Murdochs
were heavy coffee drinkers, but Uncle Heb and Uncle
Nun had drank more than she and it never kept them
awake. She could hear them sawing wood in what Granmam called "the boys' shed room." The valley roosters
had their first round of crowing till the girl slept, and it
was making daylight through the white oaks when she
woke.

Now why did a queer feeling go through her as she
spelled out what day this was coming up over Kettle
Mountain? Sunday had run through the valley plenty of
times before but not, she reflected, with what lay ahead
today. Morg Gandy's name stayed unspoken at breakfast and dinner but she knew her folks meant to hear

him. The men had on clean shirtsleeves except Granpap who carried the map of Washington County in coffee stains on his white shirt front, but he wore his gold plated collar button and that was his collar and tie. It told plainly he had dressed up proper for the occasion. Even Mam had taken off for the afternoon.

Chariter looked over them troubled. Most times it felt good trooping down the lane with her folks around her. Now wasn't it queer that today it went against her, that for once in her life she hankered to be alone? Well, she didn't know as she liked it, feeling fussy and special like her own folks weren't good enough for her. But that's the way it was. She wanted to sit in that school house private by herself today. Either that or she didn't want to go at all.

She'd have done it, too, if Babe hadn't seen her sneak off and followed her up on the old mountain road. She heard him behind her in the Tankersly cuttings.

"I ast you if I could go along, Chariter!" he bawled after.

She waited for him provoked.

"You asked but I never said you could go," she scolded when he caught up.

"I won't be no trouble, Chariter," he begged her.

"Well, come on then," she gave in. "But I don't want to hear you gabbing all the time today."

Grateful, he stumbled after her. They crossed the

cuttings where Ant Dib said a blacksnake hid under every brush pile and out into the cool of the Hocking tract. Old Mr. Hocking, who lived in Dumont, claimed it virgin timber, but Granpap said it was no such thing, only cut so long ago none could remember. All the stumps, he said, had rotted away. Uncle Nun agreed with him, said it would be pine and hemlock if it was virgin, instead of the oak and other hardwoods that came up after the softwoods were cut. Just the same it looked to Chariter like nobody had ever struck an axe in here. Every time she came it seemed like a place only the deer and the fisher fox knew. She and Babe could have been dwarfs bobbing among the big butts.

"Don't you mind it in the dark, Chariter?" Babe whimpered.

"I don't call it dark in here," she told him shortly.

The fact was she liked it in the big timber under the spell of a strange power that could set up monster butts and fix their ropy roots deep in the rocky earth. Lichens covered the mouldy old poplars far up as she could see and soft green moss healed the knots. The rock oaks had hide like alligators, but the beech was a fat tree with skin thin and smooth as an apple. Her and Babe's feet made little sound in the deep mould. Some place in here was water running. She could hear it tinkle and the long drawn out breath of the wood pewee sighing up yonder in the far away green roof.

At a thumping big white oak the road came out into second or third growth timber. Uncle Nun called it The Sprouts. You felt no wind yet the leaves of the quaking asp danced. Some said this was the tree they strung up Christ on and ever since its leaves kept shaking. The road ran clearer and plainer here and they had the sky back again while the sun on greenbriar and sassafrass leaves nigh onto blinded you.

"Chariter," Babe wanted to know. "Why does it have rattlesnakes?"

Now how could anybody answer that? she thought. She had riddle enough today. The road lay between stone fences looking strange here in the mountain, some fallen down, some standing up, most covered by creeper, sometimes with a stout tree pushed up between the rocks, scattering them here and yon. This was a flat on the mountain bench and there'd been a house once, and fields. Granpap still called it the Geyer place though he and Uncle Nun fought and argued where the house stood, for nary a trace was left, only the green bed of some kind of lilies that came up every year. Nobody knew what they were, for they'd laid there so long they'd bloomed themselves out.

"This is where them folks died of black diptheria," Chariter told Babe.

"All of them?" he quavered.

"All but him," she said. "Once he had them all buried he lit out and nobody around here seen him since."

Babe stopped to stare at the green lily bed that like the vanished house and fields would never blossom again. The girl tried to conjure up in her mind a picture of this Geyer man left so tragic alone. She had seen young ones before without a pap but never a pap without young ones.

Beyond the Geyer place the woods raised over them again. Poisonous looking red oyster shells grew on logs, and an old gray birch stood like a witch in her rags and tatters. Now the road turned down little by little with only humps up again, then down some more, till a swampy stream crossed the road. Here Chariter turned on what looked like a deer path up the mountain.

"Where you going now?" Babe complained.

"Uncle Nun took me up here once," Chariter told him.

Climbing they reached the bench again and came out in a place full of pinkster starting to bloom, a whole acre of it, some daddy trees twenty feet high, a sight to see this time of year. Uncle Nun had said there must be something in the ground just right for pinkster and that's why it swarmed with humming birds after the honey.

"You heard about this place but you never seen it," Chariter told him. "It's the hummer grove."

"I kin smell it!" Babe crowed. "But I don't see no hummers."

"Maybe they're not here yet or gone to church meeting some place," the girl said. "Uncle Nun seen them here once on a week day. It had hundreds, he said, all trying to chase the rest off like this wild place belonged to them."

They stood there taking it in for a while. If she hadn't been going anywhere, she'd have sat herself down on that log yonder and let her mind woolgather in this pretty picture place. It reminded her of that old school song for Christmas, "The angel of the Lord came down and glory shone around." She had wondered about that. Some folks, she knew, made fish bigger than they were and saw spooks in the woods when it was only some turned up windfall. But this pinkster grove here on Black Log Mountain was real for anybody to see.

"Let's stay for the hummers?" Babe begged when she turned to go.

"I want to get there early for a back seat," Chariter told him. "I don't want to stick out up in front like a blackbird in a dogberry tree."

The rest of the family wasn't around when she and Babe came sliding down through the slippery hemlock woods to the school house standing at the covered bridge. Likely they had gone back looking for her and

Babe. Outside, valley men and boys smoked and talked. Inside two back rows were already filled. The third back row had two seats left on the center end. Nobody wanted them because the stove in the middle shut off the view to the teacher's desk. Here Chariter sat herself down, putting Babe in first, for this was almost as good as the back row, hiding her behind the stove. None of her family could settle down next to her now.

"So this is where you're at?" Fox jeered when the rest showed up. They all had to traipse up in front. Ant Dib with one twin grinned at them but Granmam with the other looked stern, and Mam with Honey made as if she didn't see her. Hardly any menfolk but Vince came in, most of them preferring to stand out at the door and open windows to chew and spit and say among themselves what they wanted.

And now Chariter guessed by the unlikely quiet outside, then by grunts from the men, "How're you, Morg?" that the one Tom Leck called the cat gut scraper had come. She didn't look back but waited for his shadow to fall on her as he passed between her and the potbellied stove. Something went over her then as she felt him close, something never felt before, as if up to now she had been a Chinese jigsaw puzzle lacking one part lost a long while, but now that missing part had been found and put in its place, and she could be whole and in one piece for the first time. Then he passed and

47

pity ran over her as she saw how lame he was, going up and down on one side. But her pity took off when a woman set down her shoes hard after him and two young boys after her, one Fox's size and one Babe's, all heading for the teacher's platform where they sat down on chairs fetched up for them from the Gandys.

"Who's them two?" Babe whispered.

Chariter didn't answer. The man opened his black case, took out a fiddle and started to play, first, Will There Be Any Stars in My Crown, then We Are Going Down the Valley One By One, both pieces that Chariter liked. In between he gave a short preaching.

"Now Mrs. Gandy and our children will talk to you," he said. "Noble and Morgan, Junior, first."

The young boys came forward stiffly one at a time to tell how they were saved, each rattling off his piece like counting up to a hundred. You could tell they had done this many times before. She felt sorry for them having to stand up and say such weak made-up things like girls. But she felt no pity for the woman when it came time for her to play the preacher. Now wasn't it curious, the girl thought, that Morg Gandy had a weakness for women who yelled? It sounded almost like Mam up there bawling somebody out. The notion of Mam on the platform preaching was so droll Chariter had to shake so that Babe poked her to ask what was she laughing at? Then she froze as a kind of poison came into the wall-faced woman's voice and she said God Almighty should come like a sword in this valley and smite them living in sin.

"Especially smite the harlot!" she called out. "Her who enticed innocent men to her den, even a holy young man of the Word, and now brings up her lawless offspring without benefit of the kingdom. Shame her and fetch her forward this afternoon to confess her sins as scarlet."

Chariter looked to where her mam sat on a front bench holding Honey on her lap and never a sign that she heard. But if she didn't, her girl did, and her eyes fastened hard on this woman who had set herself up as God Almighty to judge the onetime neighbor folks of her man. The girl guessed Morg must have told her how once he had hung around Dockey Murdoch like a hummer after a pinkster flower and this had stuck in his woman's jealous craw, so now she'd have it back at that other woman the first chance she got. Only when Chariter looked at the two young boys did the flint in her soften. She told herself they couldn't help they were born lawful while she wasn't, that their father and mother had a marriage paper somewhere in a court house with the bald eagle of the country in gold atop the steeple, and a big book stowed away in the same place with the young ones' names set down not with their mother's alone but with their rightful daddy's, too, while her and Babe and Fox and Honey had only their mam's name, and what line was written where their pap's name should be, none of them knew. No, those young boys couldn't help it, but neither had they call to sit up there so big and goody-goody like they had no behinds.

Chariter never took her eyes off the baldheaded man when he came down off the platform telling folks to confess their sins and be saved. He found easy pickings with Vilet Cummings who hardly could tell you anything without crying. Calling her Sister, he led her up in front. He called Vince Foote, Brother, but Vince stayed glued to his seat, and the revival man had to give him up and come down the middle of the school room stopping and working on them with seats near the end.

This was when Chariter kicked herself for being where she was. If she'd had sense, she'd have gone to the far end of the next row where likely he'd pass her by. She noticed he'd given Mam, Granmam and Ant Dib a wide berth, knowing them well enough, but he wouldn't know her, never having seen her before, and now his eyes seized on her as easy game, stopping by her seat, calling her Sister and plying her to come up in front and tell out her sins. She turned her face off to throw cold water on him but he stuck like a leech. Uncle Nun guyed her afterward she must have looked mighty wicked but Mam said Morg Gandy always had been a fool for a pretty face and figure, and the younger the tastier. Anyhow now he wouldn't give her up, setting his sights for her, dunning her to blab out in front of everybody what she done wrong so she wouldn't have to burn through eternity like a pine knot from the devil's woodpile.

"You seen that blacksmith shop down across the crick, Sister, ah? You seen his bellows blowing up the forge? You seen the coal and iron get red hot, ah? Well, let me tell you something, Sister, ah. If you think that's hot, ah. Let me tell you if you ever fell out of hell into that red hot forge, Sister, you'd shake and shiver with the cold, ah."

Chariter reckoned that "ah" must be some blast against sin like Uncle Nun's "huf" in wood chopping. She did her best to hold her horses. She didn't want to run the first time she met the man Nobe and Effie acted like might have daddied her. But when he got down on his knees with his shoes to the potbellied stove and his violently folded hands on her lap and thighs where they had no right to be, she couldn't help looking at him in a kind of terror and shame. There his face flared hardly a foot away from hers. His red mustache looked like it had some kind of oil splashed on it, his eyes half bloodshot and his bald head burning up with the hell fire he talked about. She reckoned it was his breath she hated most, sour and foul like Granpap's when he puked up

Nicodemus's white mule. Still she sat and stuck it out, but when the lame man started moving his hands around on her hams, calling her Sister, she got to thinking it had gone on long enough.

"I'm not your sister!" she called out, giving him a crack across the face. "Nor your darter or any other relation either."

That set off Mam sitting up in front, ready to lend a hand if her girl couldn't take care of herself.

"You let her alone, Morg Gandy!" she called back. "You got plenty to do to shut up your woman's big mouth."

The man had picked himself up mighty quick and gone down the other side of the stove exhorting like before but it seemed the wind had gone out of his sails. He didn't get down on his knees by any more today. The hard eyed woman up on the platform never said a word. She must have seen this go on before. And the two young boys sat stiff as pokers, with unmoved faces.

Chariter felt thankful now that Fulliam had a funeral this Sunday and couldn't get off. No telling what he'd a done to Morg Gandy, but then maybe the man wouldn't have been so shameless with Fulliam sitting by her. She felt glad anyhow she hadn't jumped up and run out. Vince Foote and Mrs. Peeples came around afterward and said she had done right. Others did the same, while Mam stood there like a fighting cock.

"I don't know what he was doing to her," she said. "But if he was doing what I think he was, I'd a given him more'n her. That big mouthed woman of his would of heard some of the things he done around here that he wants to put on others now."

The Murdochs went down the road together. Mam planted herself on one side of Chariter and Ant Dib walked skinny and friendly on the other. Granmam gave the girl a slow look while Granpap came close behind muttering words she couldn't make out any more than Granmam's look. Some places they stretched across the road like a line of wild geese in the fall, bunching up around her when they passed a team or people, acting like somebody might make off with her. Oh, the girl recognized the tribal protection. It felt good enough, she guessed. And yet that night when she got awake it was as if something had died, something both close to and distant from her, something never had she known or now would she.

CHAPTER VI

CHARITER noticed the family let her have her way after that, treating her like a young one who'd had a bad spill. Well, they needn't. What happened at the school house didn't make her a mushroom that wasn't born one minute and the next there she'd popped up under the apple tree.

Oh, they could coddle her at home if they wanted. She reckoned she could take it without getting spoiled. Ant Dib was the one had the idea of a dandelion party. It was getting late for dandelions and that's how Chariter knew they'd done it on her account. If they'd wanted dandelions, they'd have gone for them in April or early May. Late as it was nobody said no. Even Granpappy said he'd go, but that was no wonder, since the dandelions were for wine, and Granmam made the best in the valley, pale, mild and sweet with a kick like Nicodemus's mule.

"We'll go Saturday," Ant Dib said. "Then maybe Fulliam could go along."

Chariter threw her a grateful look. She sat down that evening and spelled him out a letter on Fox's school tablet. Sure enough Fulliam got off for the weekend. He was at the door in his valley clothes Saturday morning. He and Fox took the baskets, Babe the empty flour bags, Granpap the coffee kettle. Ant Dib and Granmam each toted a twin while Chariter carried Honey when she didn't give her to Fulliam.

"He might as well get used to toting a young one," she told herself.

Most Kettle folks went to Jeffs Valley by road. The Murdochs could, too, if they wanted, in their spring wagon, three miles down the valley, one and a half miles through Bubbs Gap and three back up Jeffs Valley. But what would they want to do that for when to tramp over the mountain was hardly one mile up and one down? Besides, a path beat a road any day, nobody to mind your business, the way ever turning, a new sight by the minute, shaded generally from the sun. They trooped in single file over the Stevens bridge and by the barn and house where Dockey came out and looked after them enviously.

Oh, it made the Murdochs grin that Dockey had to work while they could go pleasuring up over the old chestnut ridge where stubs stood plenty as jaggers on a porcupine. Once those trees were a sight in flower Granmam said, and Granpap complained their powerful sweet stink nigh used to put you to sleep. You could smell it down at the barn when the wind was right. In the fall the Kitteredges had nuts on that ridge by the wagon box. But now the blight had got them. Up behind the chestnut ridge was the mountain meadow half gone back to the wild where the skyflower grew. Each blue eye had its eyewinkers around it but they didn't come out till fall when near everything else was gone. Past the meadow was Black Spring where Granpap said black cherry trees bore when he was a boy. It had fields here once, he told. Oh, he could go on all day if you wanted to listen.

From here the path went through solid woods, steeper now, turning soft and green underfoot with moss, always getting further up the mountain, sometimes with open spots where the purple velvet of birdsfoot violets looked up at you. Old timber roads crossed. Granpap knew just where to fork and where to keep on. Ranks of solid rock oak stood around and all the time the feel of the mountain under you got stronger till up ahead you could make out monster rocks through the trees and then you knew you were close to the comb with only the sky atop you and the feel of being high over Kettle Valley, Jeffs Valley and the river, the railroad, Tinsburg, Earlville, Dumont and all the places she knew.

The younger ones threw down their burdens and shinned up the rocks. Some called them the Coal Train, a string of stone cars left standing since creation. Fulliam pulled Chariter off into a rock crack. Ever since he stood at the back door this morning she could tell he had something eating him. You couldn't mistake the wilful look in his eyes or how his forelock stood up with what ran in his blood or noggin. That's when the wild part in her drew toward him the most although her head sometimes had other notions. What ate him he didn't get to tell her, for hardly had they got in the rock crack till Babe tagged after.

"Get out of here," Fulliam told him.

But Babe only went to the end of the crack.

"Come on down from those rocks before you fall down!" Ant Dib sang out down below.

"That's how your Uncle Robby got his peg leg," Granpappy yelled. "He fell down off these rocks and smashed the bone to baking powder."

"He did not," Ant Dib said vigorously. "He was sleeping off a drunk on the railroad track."

"That was another time," Granpap declared. "You better come on down, Chariter, if you don't want to go through life with a leg you can't warm up when it's cold. I mind the time me and a woman from Molleystown found your Uncle Robby laying out in zero weather. He'd had a couple of drinks and was froze stiff. He couldn't get up. I started to rub the good leg and this woman started on the peg, only she didn't know it. 'I kain't git this leg warm,' she kept on saying. 'It's froze hard as steelyards.' "

"Come on down, I tell you," Granmam called. "We're lighting out now."

Babe wouldn't go till Chariter went. Fulliam took a couple of swipes at him on the way. The path down the mountain was worn hard as the one coming up but you could tell this was the south side. Uncle Nun and Heb claimed it always warmer on this side. The snow went quicker and the leaves hung on longer. Things grew on this side you never found on the other, like the tulip laurel that got such waxy flowers and big leaves. It was dryer over here, moss scarcer. Not a place did they see where crowfoot smothered the ground like on the north side. Yet the water that came out of this side of the mountain, Granpap said, tasted with that of the other. You couldn't tell the difference though you could between this mountain and Black Log. Every mountain had its own taste, he said. Some was sweet, some was bitter and some rusted pipes and caked your insides with canker.

When they came out on the Jeffs Valley road, they didn't have to go farther. The field across the road was white with dandelion in seed and "yaller" with the weed in flower. They piled across the fence, stowed away

Honey and the twins in a hollow in the grass. The three looked snug and cozy lying together in their green bed, sociable as three young fox pups their mam had dragged out of their den in the sun. Ant Dib said she'd come back to see that no snake sneaked out of the grass to snuggle among them.

Now wasn't it a pity, the girl told herself, that Fulliam had to be off his feed today? Was he put out by what had happened to her at the school house? Well, whatever ailed him, she wasn't going to let it spoil her party. It had been like medicine to come over here today. Stay home too long and it seemed the sap faded out of living. Cross the mountain and you found it hadn't faded out on this side. The timothy looked fresh as she'd ever seen it, Granmam's blue dress as bright as the day she made it and Granpap's eyes a match. It felt mortal good just to wade through the green of the field smelling the crushed grass underfoot, reaching down to tear off the low golden heads, hoarding them in her flour sack, keeping abreast of Fulliam so he had company, coming out with small talk now and then so dandelion picking wouldn't be too piddling for him after undertaking. Once in a while she sneaked a handful into his sack that wasn't filling up fast as it ought.

"I can pick my own," he flared at her once.

"You got further to reach down than me," she said. "You don't want to come back shy."

"I got something more to think about than dandelions," he told her.

Now what did he mean by that? went through her mind. Could he have got mixed up with a woman around Earlville, she wondered, perhaps with some fresh widow pining for a good-looking young undertaker to comfort her? She threw him a sidewise cast. His Uncle Fulliam and most town men looked to her like fine stuffed suits of clothing walking down the street. But no suit of clothes could hide the man in Fulliam. If his chest showed through his coat to her, she reckoned, it likely did to other women.

Well, if that's the way it was, that's the way it would have to be, she told herself, but she didn't want to hear any of it today. She was out after dandelions and she meant to stay that way till they got back over the mountain. She watched she said nothing that might lead him to unburden himself, swapping chitchat to keep him bottled up till they got back among the rest where he couldn't spill it. Down in the hollow they were waiting for them, the littlest ones still kicking up their heels in the grass.

"Well, you got back so you did," Ant Dib said like she'd expected them to stay off for a while.

Granmam said their bunch looked like movers when they made tracks for Kettle Mountain. Granpappy claimed he knew like the back of his hand where Nun and Heb and Chick made their ties and lagging. He marched at the head with his white sack over one shoulder and the big coffee pot over the other. They went down the road about a mile and up a woods road into the mountain with the sound of axes getting closer until they came out on the landing.

"About time you come," Uncle Nun said. "We figured you got lost in the bean patch."

Granpappy overlooked that.

"Oh, we finish what we start," he told him. "Like Uncle Robby, the time he found the chickens ate his watermelon seeds. He just cut their gizzards open, took out his seeds and sewed them up again. Them seeds gave the tastiest watermelons he ever ate and it didn't hurt the chickens none either."

Granmam sent Babe with the big coffee pot for run water. Ant Dib started a fire. The uncles got out their kettles. Granmam opened the baskets and pretty soon they were sitting around on fresh-hewn ties and fresh-split laggings instead of chairs and benches, with a pile of bright sweet-smelling chips for a table. Chick jiggled first Jess then Jessie on his knee, feeding them slivers of ham fat from his kettle. The coffee smelled good and tasted better over here. Uncle Nun kept brushing the crumbs off his mustache.

At home they generally ate in a hurry and no talk. The men hardly even said "Pass the bread." They just reached out with their forks and stabbed themselves a piece. But they didn't have company in the woods every day. Besides this was Saturday noon and they were quitting. Chariter never saw Granpap so peart.

"This lunch minds me of the free lunch we had one night at the Red Lion," he told. "Me, Uncle Robby and Al Creedle. Al drank a little more than he could carry and me and Uncle Robby went out and changed the wheels of his spring wagon around. Then we hitched up the horses hind-foremost. They were baldfaced sorrels and when Al came out and crawled up in the seat, he seen them white face horses standing there looking at him. He gave out a holler. He thought he had the skeevers. Uncle Robby and me had to hitch them horses right end forrard and Al druv away with one side of his wagon rifting up and down."

Granpap scrambled up over the piles of mine sills and laggings, saying what was up to snuff and what wasn't.

"Listen to the tie inspector," Uncle Nun jeered.

"You kin be glad I'm not inspecting. I'd throw half this kindling out," Granpappy said.

All the time Chariter could feel Fulliam itching beside her. He told in her ear to go off in the bush like she had to go on business and meet him where the little run came out of the gap. She was waiting behind a dogberry when he got there.

"I had to tramp half the mountain to lose them

brothers of yours," he said. "I hope that Babe stays lost all night."

The run was a branch of Jeffs Creek coming down the hollow between the Little Mountain and Kettle. It went through a race course of boulders, some high as a man, most round as a ball and coated with moss. The water made pretty music. Here on the green bank Fulliam could say freely what was eating him.

"Me and my Uncle Fulliam had a fall out," he told her.

So it wasn't a woman after all, the girl thought. Well she didn't know which was worse. She and him had always counted on Uncle Fulliam. Why, ever since Fulliam was a little fellow he had told how his uncle was taking him in the business some day and leaving it to him when he died, since he had no young ones and Fulliam was his namesake. And now already Fulliam was sick of it.

"I thought you liked working on bodies," she said.

"If I made as much as he does, I would," he told her. "But I still got to go to embalming school to get license. He won't get me a machine hearse. I have to feed and shine up his old horses, and clean out the stable. If somebody I never even heard of drops dead, I got to get out there night or day like the body was going to run away. Every funeral old women hand me bunches of roses that bleed my hands like rattlesnakes. If it rains at the cemetery, I got to give my rain coat to the poor widow and get soaked myself. And I don't get enough to keep a dog, let alone a woman."

"I guess it takes time, Fulliam," she said sadly. "World wasn't made in a day."

"No, but it would a been if it'd been me making it," he declared. "I'd a done it before breakfast and moved over the mountain before dinner time."

"Well, I hope you're not quitting till you get something else," she said.

"I got it already," he told her. "I figure to work here in the woods with Nun and Heb. They took Chick in. They can take me. Then you and me could be together."

So it was a woman after all, she said to herself, and she was the woman. Her face set.

"I guess you know what your pap'd say?"

"I don't care what he says. If he don't want me at his place I could stay at yours. It's always got room for one more. Then me and you could be together all the time. In the night time, too."

The girl's eyes grew cruel and her mouth ropey. So that's what he was thinking? Well, she was nothing for it. She had no notion to let herself follow her mam and Ant Dib. First thing she'd know she'd have a young one at her skirts and then another and not a marriage paper for her or her young ones either. No, she'd seen too much of such business. She held herself more than that, and if she didn't, she would for her young ones. She wasn't going to bring them in the world unlawful if she could help it. They weren't going to cast it up to her some day that she hadn't done right by them.

"I'm not for letting you bury yourself in the woods," she let him know.

His eyes threw her a dark look. Oh, you're not, are you? they said. Well, wait till I tell you how it is. Then you can do as you please and so can I.

"I've thought this thing through," he told her. "If you won't go along with me, I know somebody who will."

Chariter stood there stolidly. So she was right the first time, and the woman was somebody else. Well, this is what you got in life, what you got born for, to see how much you could take and what you were going to do about it. A lot more women than her must have had the same put up to them in their day. She saw Fulliam watching her. He figured he had her now. And if he didn't, she was close enough to work to his will.

Now wasn't it strange, the girl thought, it had got so quiet in here? It seemed like the run had slowed down. She told herself she'd never seen a seemlier courting place. The spicewood bushes closed them in. The big level white oak branches hung low like a roof overhead. The moss lay soft and green on the bank save where it showed black from Fulliam's heels. The run gave out soft music. The little birds came hopping down from rock to rock to drink and douse their feathers.

"Are you telling me you want to break off?" she put to him.

"I didn't settle down with you yet," he pointed out. You could see he thought he had her. "I still have my ruthers."

"What's her name?" she asked him, curious.

He gave a start.

"Who? Oh, her?" He threw up his head. "Her name's Maybel."

Maybel, Maybel, she repeated to herself. There was Maybel Winter up the valley. She'd always reckoned it a pleasing name, but something deceitful hung to it now. She got ready to go. The rest must be looking for them this long time.

"Well, if them's your ruthers, Fulliam, you'll have to take them," she said. It came in her mind to tack on that if this Maybel would take him at his terms she wasn't much account, but that would be calling her own mam and ant no account. She'd better hold her tongue. It had gone bad enough. No use making it worse. It always had somebody in the world like this Maybel, whoever she was, to make a fool of herself if she wanted.

CHAPTER VII

THE dandelion party would have done something for Chariter, she guessed, if Fulliam hadn't hung that millstone around her neck. Now she reckoned she'd lost a man and a pap in one week. But if Fulliam wanted to live his life with this Maybel, whoever she might be, that was his rights, like hers if she didn't want Morg Gandy for a daddy. The same week Tom Leck called to her across the crick from the door of his blacksmith shop when she and Fox went by with the egg baskets.

"Stop at the house sometime."

"What do you want?" Fox wanted to know.

"I'm not talking to you. I mean Chariter," the blacksmith said when they came over the bridge. He gave the girl a friendly look from under his bushy eyebrows. She'd noticed he acted especially close to her since the meeting at the school house.

Chariter said she'd stop sometime. She knew his

house was a mess with no woman to redd it up. House-hold stuff and rattle traps stood piled to the ceiling with only cowpaths through to the stove, bed and back door basin. A lot of his stuff he bought at public sales. He'd close up shop any time to go to a vendue. He said he couldn't let something go for a couple of cents when he could fix it up and get a couple of dollars for it. Only, he never got time to work for himself, he claimed. They ran him ragged at the shop.

"Don't come too soon. I got to fix it up a little first," he said.

"I thought," Fox jeered, "you were going to fix up that junk long ago."

"I'm a doing it," the blacksmith said. "Just give me time. The Lecks is master smiths and always was. They kin do anything with wood or iron. Sip's the same way."

"How about that Leck over in Porter Valley that mumbles?" Fox taunted him.

"Nothing the matter with Jake save his tongue," Tom said quickly. "The Lord missed hanging it right. Even so his mumbling's better than a good many's talk. You mightn't catch on to every word but you can spell out what he's aiming at. He runs up and down like a sam. When he runs up, you know it's something you better listen to. When he runs down, you don't need to give much notice. But when he runs up and down both

68

and holds in the middle, you know he's satisfied and singing like a sam in church."

"I heerd him once and couldn't make out no sam," Fox said.

"Oh, he might slight his words sometimes," Tom allowed. "But he's a master hand with tools like all the Lecks and don't you forget it. He kin fix up anything, even pocket watches. He once made one of them long weight clocks all by hisself. You know the kind that sets on the floor and stands higher than a man's head. He cut down and ripped up his own walnut, painted the face out of the bottom of an old bucket, hammered out the hands and cut out a piece of galvanized iron for the moon to come up. The whole works he made or put together hisself from truck he had or parts he blacksmithed. It worked true as preaching, told the time of day, the day of the week and month, and the cast of the moon. Oh, a lot of folks came around just to lay eyes on that clock, Chariter, and still do, I guess. I heered one say it could talk plainer than Jake could, but he never had nothing the matter with him save his tongue."

He seemed anxious to reassure Chariter.

"No Leck ever had to be ashamed of his name," he told her. "No scrofula like runs in the Childers and comes out on their faces. No fits like the Hills. A Leck was once head man for the old Porter furnace. This was way back. General Washington claimed they made the best iron in the country for cannon. They used to wagon it down with manure on the top to get it through the British lines."

Chariter pricked up her ears a little. Tom went on.

"Yes, the Lecks way back were all master smiths. They say Sip's the best in Dumont to take an auto machine apart and put it together."

Chariter had heard other things about Sip but not from Tom. They said he and his mother fought like cat and dog when he came home. Granmam said it was over that machine of his he hadn't paid for yet. More than once this year Chariter and Babe had seen him driving it up from the stone bridge, looking great shakes sitting at the wheel, the dust flying, the black top shivering in the wind.

"What does he have to have a machine for?" Granmam said. "He lives where it has trolleys if he don't want to walk. A machine eats more than hay," she went on significantly. "And Sip ought to know better than try to get money out of Wichita. She's tight as the bark on a tree. She don't even believe in banks since he forged on her. She'd sooner trust an old sauerkraut or apple butter crock in the cellar."

Chariter knew that but didn't want to think about it today. Tom was a nice old man and a master hand with tools. The bad they said about Sip and his mam could take a back seat. It was like Uncle Nun said the time he hunted rabbits on Squire Goddem's posted land. "Didn't you see my signs, Nun?" the squire asked him. "I wasn't hunting signs, Squire. I was hunting rabbits," Uncle Nun told him. Well, she wasn't hunting bad about the Lecks right now. Most every man, she reckoned, had his dark side of the moon. It went back to Adam. It's what made him a man.

She heard only good about Sip once she and Fox got to Wichita's place. A short visit for eggs wasn't long enough for talk the woman had stored up since last time. She kept after the girl to stay all night. Fox could take the eggs and go to the Gandys. What did she want to go up there for anyhow? The girl put her off. Talk about Sip satisfied something inside, but she didn't hanker to sleep in his mam's bed. She had done it a couple of times and Wichita took up most of the tick, hollowing it down so the girl had to lay on the rim and watch she didn't roll down hill. Her bed at home had a hole in it, too, but if Fox or Babe got in first, she could lift him out after he was asleep and get in the hole herself. She couldn't do that with Wichita.

Today Sip's mam sent Fox out to gather the eggs and carry water so she had more time with Chariter. She never let up talking whether up and around or letting her weight back gingerly to her quivering rocker.

"From the time he was little, Chariter, that boy liked nice things. He always said he wanted to be a clock-smith and jewelry man with finger rings and diamonds in the showcase. And then Tom had to take him down to his dirty old shop and get his hands black and his clothes full of holes from the sparks. And now all he does is lay under one of them auto machines with oil dropping in his hair and grease blobbing up his clothes. Oh, he washes up to drive around in his own machine. He takes care of it like it was a watch. I want him to give you a ride in it next time he comes out."

"I can walk," Chariter said.

"No, you come over this Sunday afternoon," Wichita told her. "I have a feeling he'll be home."

Chariter had to promise to be on hand for the ride. She would have, too, if something hadn't got ahead of her. And that something was the big black dog Gran-mam said runs ahead of Death. She didn't see the dog but she did Russell Allyn's woman running up the path from the shop. It was Sunday and the shop was closed.

"Tom here?" she hollered still a ways off. "His woman's lying murdered on her kitchen floor."

Chariter always knew she could stir her stumps. More than once her feet had left Fox and Babe behind. But never before today did she reckon she could put so much ground between her and the rest.

"Wait on us, Chariter!" Ant Dib called after. "The hellhound who done it might be still laying around."

The girl let up a little then, making sure to keep only a couple of fence rails ahead of the others. She flew up the hill through the pine woods and across Wichita's oats field. The first thing she looked for was Sip's machine in the wagon shed where he kept it on a Saturday night but it wasn't there. Maybe he hadn't come this week. Now she slowed down, for she could see across the garden fence where Wichita's door stood open and still.

Once past the draw well, she didn't run. Only a step at a time she took over the rickety porch and into the kitchen that always had the same warm yeasty smell like nobody else's house. Today the smell was faint and the room cold. The rest of the kitchen looked the same, the old red table cloth, the time-worn cherry cupboard, the bare spot on the wall where the ancient paper had peeled and the big silent rocking chair with its thin "yaller" cushion. She saw the teeter still swinging from the clock on the shelf, the dipper floating in the bucket half full of water, and then on the other side of the table the mountain of woman lying on the floor by the cellar door. Her head didn't look natural, hanging to one side with an ugly lump on the low forehead. The girl reached down to touch a cheek. It was white and hard as gravestone. She reckoned she would never lay in the same bed with that pile of flesh again. No, from now on Wichita would have to sleep alone.

Uncle Nun came blowing through the door.

"Get away there, girl," he warned. "Let everything set till Tom gets here."

It was strange to come out of the house and see Wichita's chickens roaming lively over the place as if their mistress wasn't lying in there gone from this world, and to see Star cropping the grass like nothing had happened. Chariter reckoned she'd better milk her, for it looked like Wichita had been dead since last night. The cow's tits stood out like master thumbs. The girl was still there and so was most everybody else from this end of the valley when the sheriff showed up. Still she hung around thinking that Fulliam might come with his uncle to tend to the body. But the sheriff told Tom he had phoned an undertaker in Dumont.

"Now you tell Fulliam how it was so he don't blame me," Tom told Chariter.

"If I see him ahead of you, I'll tell him," the girl said. No use giving more. Let Tom and the valley find out for their selves that she and Fulliam had broken off.

Tom didn't do much mourning. He went around sober as a man should with his woman dead from hitting the stove with her head when she was pushed or knocked over. Nobody looked for him to show grief since he and Wichita had been on the outs all these years. The only time anything came out on him, and then it wasn't grief, was when he saw all those crocks with their wooden lids scattered over the cellar floor. He climbed back to the kitchen and those that were there felt sorry for him, all but Granpap.

"I tole him," Granpap said. "I tole him long ago."

"What did you tell him, you old bushnipple?" Ant Dib said.

"I tole him the time Sip forged his mam's name to that note. I tole him that's what he got for letting his boy larn to fool with pen and paper."

Ant Dib looked away.

"I'm waiting," she said, "to see if Sip comes to the funeral."

"It'll take brass to do that," Granmam said.

Vince Foote reckoned he wouldn't show up. Or, if he did, the sheriff would be with him.

"I heered the sheriff took him in and let him go," Heb said.

"He took him in to talk to him," Uncle Nun told them. "He had nothing to hold him on, they said. No-body seen him come and nobody seen him go."

"Some heard a machine in the night," Ant Dib said.

"Hearing don't count. The only one might a seen him was Tom, and you kain't expect him to tell on his own boy."

"He'll never show up," Vince repeated. "Not in front of us around here who know what went on."

But those who doubted had to eat their words. The afternoon of the burying Sip came up the lane in his machine and into the house bold as could be, a jack-a-dandy in his fine new-bought suit of clothes. He sat with Tom never moving an eye winker at what the Tinsburg preacher said about his mam or at all the lonesome singing. It gave Chariter a queer feeling to see him there bare faced only a couple of feet away from her, each of his black hairs combed in place, and all the time Wichita laid out in full view in her coffin. At times through the preaching the girl could hear the dead woman's geese calling. She thought they called not to their mistress but to her sitting in the hot close room. "Hank, hank, hank!" they went like they were mocking at her. "Now who do you think you are?" they said. "You got only what was coming to you."

Home in bed that night she solaced herself best she could. For one thing, she needn't wonder anymore what folks she had on the Leck or any other side. She had enough on her mam's side to stand by her rain or shine. Come to think of it, she didn't know as she needed any more. She had done without all her young life. She reckoned she could go on lacking them now when she pushed sixteen.

But wasn't it a pity that the sheriff had been so fore-

handed looking out for an undertaker friend and Fulliam's uncle hadn't got the funeral. Otherwise, she'd
have had a look at Fulliam. Folks said he was still in
Earlville. Fact is she'd likely have got a look at him
twice, once in the house and once at the graveyard. She
could have told the way he looked how he was making
out without her. Had he come, they might even have
had a word or two between them.

CHAPTER VIII

Now who would have thought that of all her folks it was Granpappy she could blame for opening up the piece of luck laying ahead in her life? And his toothache was the start of it.

It came on him Saturday. That night he went out to Nicodemus for mule to licker it away. But Nicodemus was off on business and Granpappy went to town, never getting back till Sunday evening, his face swelled out either from the tooth or fighting on the way. Heb put him to bed but Granmam said they weren't done with him yet. Sure enough in the short hours of the night he sobered up and came down waking everybody in the place, yelling for Dib to make him a poultice of bread and vinegar and when that didn't help, for Nun to go out and get him a fresh butchered weasel skin so he could put the bloody side to his jaw.

"How kin I find a weasel in the night time?" Nun complained.

"That's the time a weasel goes out!" Granpap yelled. "I could do it my own self if I didn't have this misery."

He was going for fair now. Oh, had he a family as big as a rooster he'd have found something for each one to do, a coffin nail for his bad tooth to bite on, a string that three mice had been hanged on, and if that failed, the sure remedy of peeing against his cheek. The stronger and hotter the pee, the quicker it would kill the toothache. They'd have been in an uproar all night if Uncle Nun hadn't had a quart of town whiskey salted away. That was better than a weasel skin or fresh pee, Chariter reckoned, for it started settling Granpap down. Uncle Nun and Heb got him back to his shanty. They came down gapping loudly. They said Granpap was dead to the world in his bed.

It was like a graveyard the rest of the night. Next morning Granmam told them to step and talk easy.

"Let sleeping dogs lay," she said.

So they all went light on their feet and soft on what they spoke. The shanty was a good ways off but Granmam said he could hear them rift down here. After dinner time Nun's whiskey must have run out, for Granpap came down to the house teetering like a gandersnipe, his cheek like a monster chew was in it, his hair a sparrow's nest.

"Ain't you better yet?" Granmam scolded him.

"Where's Nun and Heb?" Granpap wanted to know.

"Where they're always at—cutting laggin," Granmam said. "And that's where you could be if you wasn't so old and lazy."

Granpap gave her an angry look.

"Who's going to Nicodemus for me?"

"You had enough," Granmam said.

"Don't you go telling me what I had or hadn't!" Granpap warned her.

"I kin tell you one thing," Granmam said. "That tooth's coming out. And I'm the one to do it if you don't do it your own self."

"How kin I eat with my one good tooth out of business?" Granpap demanded.

They had it out hot and heavy. Granpap made the most noise but it was Granmam who won out like generally.

"Dib, you take him down to the shop," she ordered. "Tell Tom he has to pull that rotten stump. And don't let him go to Tinsburg and get drunk again."

"I ain't been drunk!" Granpap hollered.

"No," Granmam said. "And you wasn't drunk, I guess, the time you went out after pole beans and hollered, 'Dockey, come out and get me. I'm lost in the bean patch.' And neither was you the time at Dan's tavern when you had to go out and you put your shirt down instead of your pants? You know what I done to Uncle Robby the time I found him drunk in the cow stable! I put the manger chain around his neck and let him holler after he sobered up. Well, that's what I'm waiting to do to you."

Granpap's eyes retreated into his head. On no account, he said, would he go to any damned horse's hireling for his tooth pulling. And that's the way he stayed till Ant Dib said she thought Tom kept a bottle of Indian Pain Killer in the shop. Then he was willing to go, but only by fits and starts, changing his mind, kept on the road by Ant Dib and Chariter. It reminded the girl of when they'd take the cow to Dunkleberger's bull. The cow would go and then she wouldn't, her head full of notions to bolt the lane and ford the crick. In the end they always got her to the Dunklebergers and in the end they got Granpap across the crick to the blacksmith shop.

"You might have to wait a while," Ant Dib told him, noticing the horses and mules hitched outside.

"Not me," Granpap said. "He's going to get me out of my misery right now or I want to know why."

They had no need to pull him anymore. He pushed on ahead into the shop where two or three valley men loafed. Tom Leck was bent over, a mule's hoof between his legs and the cleft leather apron. He didn't look up, only grunted when Ant Dib spoke to him.

"Tom! Listen!" Granpap yelled.

Tom kept on taking horseshoe nails out of his mouth and driving them in, clinching, biting them off with the nippers. He gave the shoe a couple of approving taps, let the hoof down, straightened up halfways and took a look at his caller.

"Did the yellow jackets get you, Culy?"

"I'll yellow jacket you!" Granpap bawled.

"It's his tooth, Tom," Ant Dib said. "Mam wants you to pull it."

"Well," Tom said, I guess I kin if he holds still, but he has to wait till I get through with these mules." He spoke to the beast soothingly and picked up another hoof.

"You'd let an old broken down jackass ahead of me?" Granpap demanded.

Nig Ferrebee, owner of the animal, stepped out.

"Who are you calling a jackass?"

"Nig was here first, Culy," Tom said.

"Git out of my way!" Granpap yelled. "I'm going home."

"Don't you have some pain killer for his tooth till you get around to him, Tom?" Ant Dib said.

"I ain't a going to stand in turn with mules and jackasses!" Granpap declared.

"They was mules standing outside the shop already when I got here this morning," Tom told him.

"Well, I'm ahead of all of them!" Granpap informed him. "I had this plagued toothache yesterday already. I would a come down but you won't keep open on Sunday."

"Nig's mule had his plagued hoofache before that," Tom said. "But he kept it to hisself and never said nothing."

Granpap was boiling and steaming now.

"If you're going to count me in with mules, Tom Leck, you know what you kin do. I'm going where they ain't none. I should a never left in the first place." This time Chariter and Ant Dib had to fight to keep him.

The blacksmith watched, resigned.

"Maybe you'd let me take him, Nig, and get him out of here?"

"If it was me," Nig agreed sourly, "I'd knock out his tooth with a sledge."

The blacksmith dropped his nippers and pried Granpap's mouth open with grimy hands.

"Hold on!" Granpap yelled with pain. "I'm not Nig's mule."

"I got to see where it's plaguing you."

"You don't need to break my jaw!" Granpap hollered. "I'll show you where it's at."

The blacksmith turned and shoved a piece of steel in the fire, pumping the bellows till the sparks flew and the orange bed of the fire deepened.

"What you doing that for?" Granpap called out, alarmed.

"Just getting something ready for the mule," Tom said. He left the forge, tied a stout cord to the horn of the anvil and then to Granpap's offending tooth. "Now stand still while I temper this steel," he told him, went to the fire, took out the steel, gave it a few resounding taps with the hammer, then suddenly thrust the red-hot point at the face of Granpap who jerked back hard. It gave the anvil a heave but left the tooth still in.

"Damn you, Tom Leck and your deilish scheming!" Granpap danced with pain. He slashed the string with his knife.

The blacksmith looked sad.

"Well, I reckon we got to do it the hard way." He picked up the nippers. "Open your mouth, Culy."

Granpap closed his jaws tight.

"You're not putting them dirty, stinking mule nippers in my mouth!"

"Don't you know a mule's antiseptic?" the blacksmith told him. "That's why he kain't catch nothing."

"Well, you're not doing it without giving me some pain killer?" Granpap said, outraged.

The blacksmith sighed, went to his pile of old iron

and fished out a half empty pint bottle. Granpap put back his head and drank slowly, appreciatively, putting off his operation as long as he could, acting like Honey when she had to go to bed. He dropped the empty bottle.

"Now mind, I still got feeling!" he warned.

Tom Leck set a box on one side of the mule and Granpap on the box, then he took the other side.

"You kin brace your knees under her belly and take holt of her withers," he said. "But don't carry on or you'll scare her."

He took a vice-like grip with his huge nippers and started to put pressure on the tooth, easy at first, then with hard jerks that raised Granpap, yelling and kicking, off his box and over the back of the raring mule.

"Lemme loose!" Granpap hollered, but the blacksmith wasn't going to give up now. No, Granpap had asked for a tooth out and that's what he was going to get if Tom Leck had to drag him around the shop, which he did, and douse him in the cooling tub which he'd have liked to do but didn't. The second time around Nig Ferrebee and Johnny Little got hold of Granpap and held him till something gave.

Tom held up the tooth in his nippers triumphantly.

"A slick job if I do say it myself," he said, grinning at the men. "You feel better, Culy?"

"Better!" Granpap foamed red at the mouth. He

stood there groaning and spitting blood. "You done me meaner than Robby the time he pulled the wings off the wasps and put them in my bed."

"Now that's enough, Pappy," Ant Dib said. "Tom done you a favor."

"I'm not beholden to him," Granpap told her, spitting a scarlet stream. "Likely I'll bleed to death before I get home. If I done right by him I'd fix him so he'd pull no more teeth. He's got no license anyhow. It feels like he left half the roots in. I won't forget this in a hurry."

"Come on home, you ungrateful old bushnipple," she said.

Granpap gave Ant Dib a look.

"I'm getting outa here and I don't need you along." He turned to the blacksmith. "I ain't finished with you yet, making a fool outa me."

He was still in a lather when Chariter and Ant Dib got home. The swelling on his face went down some that afternoon but not the one in his spleen. What Tom had done to him in front of those men stuck in his gullet like a piece of persimmon skin. He kept telling how it would be if he had to do it again. The middle of the afternoon he sent Fox up to the shanty for his hat.

"The one with the GAR badge on," he called after.

"Where you think you're going?" Ant Dib demanded.

"None of your business," Granpap said. "I'm just a going."

"You're not going back to Tom's?" She put to him darkly.

"I'll go where I want to," Granpap defied her. "I only hope them fellers are still at the shop to see what I give him." Fox came running down with Great Uncle Matt's hat with the bronze badge pinned sidewise on the crown. "Give me that hat," he said, snatching it and starting off.

"You stay home before you get in trouble," Granmam said, barring his way.

"Get out of my road, Lop Ear!" Granpap warned her.

"You're going no place any more today, Culy," Granmam said and held him.

"Leggo of me!" he hollered and when she wouldn't, he bit her on the arm. When the blood showed through Granmam's sleeve, Chariter knew he had gone too far.

"Give me a hand, Dib," she said grimly. "Unlock the granary door, Chariter," she ordered.

"You'll wish you hadn't, girl!" Granpap shouted. "I'll hold you responsible. You'll get paid off like this old hellcat you all come from."

Chariter paid no attention, getting the key from a string around Granmam's neck. She opened the spring lock. Granmam and Ant Dib threw Granpap inside and

Chariter snapped the lock. He must have picked himself up in a hurry, for he started pounding the door, demanding they let him out, making the most violent threats against them all.

"Listen to him," Granmam told the young ones. "Next time he comes wheedling and truckling to you to do something for him, you kin remember what he said about you."

She went back to the house with Ant Dib while the younger ones stood around all ears to Granpap. He sure could make a racket in there, kicking, pounding, promising hell and damnation once he got loose. But the granary was double-boarded, thief-proof and rat-proof, and Granpap was still in there when Uncles Nun and Heb and Chick came home. Uncle Nun listened critically.

"He holds his age good," he said. "He couldn't holler any better when I was a little feller. Minds me of the time the wind blowed Uncle Robby's door shut and busted his jug. Uncle Robby gave that door a dressing, kicked it off its hinges so the cow run off."

The men liked their supper the minute they got home from the mountain. Usually Granmam sat down with them, but she held back tonight. You could see she wasn't herself with Granpap still locked in the granary.

"It sounds like he's settled down, Nun," she relented.

"Tell him he can come down and eat his supper if he behaves hisself."

"I'll let the old bushnipple out," Ant Dib said, and took the key. She came back shortly. "He flew outa there like a bat out of a hornet's nest. He said he don't want no supper. He still has his dander up."

"Where is he now?" Granmam wanted to know, and when Ant Dib said he had lit off through the woods she sent Fox down to tell Tom to keep an eye open for him. Fox came back and reported the shop closed. He had to tramp all the way to Wichita's house where Tom had gone back to live now, but Tom must be off some place.

"Well, that saves a fight tonight," Granmam said, relieved.

It was a pity, Chariter thought, that Granmam couldn't keep her relief, and the rest of them, too. They were sitting around the kitchen table bunching onions for market when Fox called from outside. He said something looked mighty funny. The sun went down all right but now it was coming up again. They stepped out and saw what he meant, a red light down the valley. At first it was no more than a moon tangled in the trees. Then it got bigger and started to shoot sparks.

"It looks like Nig Ferrebee's place," Uncle Heb said.

"It's nearer. It's Russel Allyn's," Granmam put in doubtfully.

"Or Tom's," Uncle Nun declared.

"God Almighty, don't say that!" Granmam told him.

Uncles Nun and Heb left at once, Chick and Fox with them. They went through the woods now almost bright as day, traveling direct for the light. It was a long time till they came back, this time by the road. All was out then but a faint glow. The smell of black smoke hung strong on them, their faces sober.

"Whose was it?" Ant Dib put to them first.

"Tom's," Nun said shortly.

"Just the barn?" Granmam hoped.

"At first," Uncle Nun said.

"Not the house, too?" Granmam begged him.

"Tom used to brag how handy that house was to the barn," Uncle Nun told. "He always said why would Charley Furst build a barn such a ways up hill from his house? I guess now he wishes his own place had been laid out like that."

"The house, too?" Granmam kept saying to herself like she couldn't believe it. Chariter didn't remember her face so ragged and gray. Why, no matter the high water, Granmam had always been the rock that stood in the middle of the crick. The flood had to go around her.

It grew late but none of them went to bed. They sat around the kitchen table drinking coffee and waiting. Nobody spoke the name but all knew whom they were waiting for. About one o'clock he showed up. Likely he'd have gone straight to his shanty if it hadn't been for the tantalizing smell of black coffee on the night air. He made a show of coming in like usual.

"You folks still up?" he said mild and mealy mouthed.

"Where were you at, Culy?" Granmam demanded sternly.

"Me? I was down at Tinsburg. I had to get something for this danged tooth."

"Why wasn't you at the fire?" Uncle Nun asked.

"I never knowed nothing about it."

Granmam turned on him a cruel face.

"So you never knowed nothing about it, Hercules Murdoch? Like you never knowed nothing about them other barns that went up in smoke. But this time you went too far."

"What are you talking about?" Granpap looked injured.

"You couldn't find Tom to fight with so you took it out on his barn!" Dockey told him.

"And after him pulling your tooth for you!" Ant Dib reproached him.

"I wouldn't do nothing like that to Tom," Granpap whined. "You know I wouldn't. Besides, you kin swear I was right here all the time."

"Not this time," Granmam's face was iron flannel. "I'm not swearing any more where you weren't. They can do that for you where you claim you were down at Tinsburg."

"Well, Dib will," Granpap wheedled. He seemed a bit shocked by the hard look on Ant Dib's face. "How about you, Dockey? You know I never done nothing like that? Well, Chariter seen me here at home all night tonight, didn't you, Chariter?" The girl didn't say anything. Something rose up in her like it had that day long ago when she was little. She had thought the sun rose and set on her granpappy then. She'd found his boots gray and scuffed one day and blacked them with stove polish while he slept off some tippling. Then she had set them by his bed and hung around to see his pleasure when he found them. Not a word did he say when he put them on, only went out in the barnyard and trampled those shiny black boots up and down in manure while she watched and something died inside of her. Well, that's the way she felt for him now and he must have seen it for he turned away. His eyes ran over one after the other. They sat around the table looking at him with stony silent faces. His confidence faded. "You'd all side with Tom against your poor old pappy," he reviled them. "If I had to do it again, never would I a spawned you."

Granmam gazed at him with bitter contempt.

"You, Culy Murdoch! You wouldn't a stopped doing what you wanted, not for God Almighty hisself."

CHAPTER IX

ALL that day Chariter looked for Tom to come with a shotgun after Granpap, but no sign of him, only of Nig Ferrebee, the constable, with a paper he said he had to give to Cully himself. Granmam sent him up to the shanty and he came down presently, Granpap along with him full of indignation and abuse.

"I'll have to take him in till the hearing unless he puts up ten dollars," Nig told Granmam.

She went in the house and came out with the money. Oh, you could tell by her face when she looked at Granpap that she didn't feel any softer toward him today than last night; but nobody was going to say she wouldn't bail her own man. Granpap tried to stop her. He wouldn't put up a dollar for dirty business like this, he said. He'd sooner go to jail. His conscience was clean as a cat's whiskers. This was Tom Leck's doing, an outrage, just to make him pay for getting his tooth pulled.

Nig listened a while, then went off with the ten dollars. That didn't stop Granpap. He was like a hound dog on an old trail, going over the track again and again, first one way and then the other, lifting up his head and baying all the time, making a slew of excitement over nothing but a rabbit last night in the cornfield. What riled him most, he said, was the paper Nig had brought. It said that he, Hercules Murdoch, with malice aforethought had stolen in that barn with coal oil to start a fire. Why, if he'd a wanted to do something like that, he wouldn't "a snuck" in. No, he would have walked right in like a man which he had full right to do after what Tom done to him in the blacksmith shop. And never would he have used coal oil. It only showed how false the whole thing was that he'd need such in a barn of all places where it didn't take more than a handful of hay or rye straw to start a fire. Listening to him, Chariter thought how a dozen bad things might be true about a man, but say one piddling part a mite off, and that man would raise the roof over how he was wronged and lied about.

The hearing was set for Saturday at Squire Goddem's. The Murdochs no more thought of working that day than Sunday. Chariter's mam at first said she'd never go up there but when the time came it looked

like she couldn't stay away. They all struck up the road
together. The Goddem place lay up the valley. From
there on all land, fields and woods belonged to the Goddems. Uncle Nun said they owned from mountain to
mountain and up to the far county line. Most of it was
in timber. That was why the first Goddem had come to
Kettle Valley, for charcoal to sell to the forges and
furnaces. But he made most of his money sawmilling,
and his sons and grandsons ever since, that and selling
timber to the mines. Old Major Goddem had built the
house. Mrs. Heller told how when she was a slip of a
girl, rich folks used to still come out from Dumont and
Baltimore to visit at the mansion house. By day they had
fox hunts and by night they dyked themselves out in
low neck finery just to sit down and eat their supper.

Oh, the name of Goddem was a power here in the old
days. But times had changed. The virgin timber was
gone, the woodlands second or third growth now, the
stone mill houses rented out to lesser folks, the old mill
boarding house turned into a rabbit warren for three
families. Once a slew of men's names made up the Goddem payroll. Now the squire paid only Harrison Laird
to work his fields and tend the stock, leasing his timber
lands to others.

But the place still held something she didn't know
what for Chariter. Looking down the hemlock lane
gave her a world of feeling. You couldn't see much

from the road, but she was going to get a real look at everything today. The Murdoch tribe pushed down between the old hemlocks, sobered by the sight of a house big as the Dumont mansions along the river. It had a heavy stone wing on one side and the same on the other. Great window frames with small panes stared out plenty as blackberries. On one side hung a roof for carriages to drive under. In back stood another fine stone house that Uncle Nun said was the stable. A stretch of shortgrass ran to the creek.

In the Squire's office they found, among others, Nig Ferrebee and two men whose barns had burned one time or another. They wanted to see how Culy Murdoch made out this time. The office looked like a school room with pictures of George Washington and Abraham Lincoln on the wall, books on shelves around three sides, a chair and desk at one end, and benches filling up the rest. Tom Leck up in front gave Granpap a hard look and Granpap a harder one back to him. Let either say a word, Chariter guessed, and they'd be at each other's throats. The only one who didn't seem to give a hait what went on in here today was the Squire himself, a self-sufficient man with sharp eyes over fierce gray mustaches that flowed in riffles like the creek above the Stevens's bridge. He sat at his desk scratching with a pen in a thick leatherbound book, the flag on a little varnished pole standing over him. The Murdochs filed in sullenly. You could see how they felt about this man and place that could send you to jail or court trial.

Now wasn't it too bad that when the Squire read out loud the long complaint of arson, Honey started to fret. The twins, one on Ant Dib's lap, one on Granmam's, stayed good as gold. But Honey was on her mam's lap and Chariter guessed what ailed her. Oh, ever since that young one came in the world it seemed she could tell when dander or tenterhooks dug into her mam. It was almost like she still lay curled up inside her like a fern leaf before it opened, her tender young flesh one with her mam's flesh. She mightn't be able to read writing yet, Granmam said, but she could read her mam's "narve strings." They must have been screwed up mighty tight in here today. Another minute and the chit was crying out for fair. Mam tried to shut her up and only made her worse.

Squire Goddem looked sharp over his mustaches.

"You'll have to remove that child," he ordered.

Now who wanted to miss what went on in here today? Not Chariter and not Chariter's mam though she had looked defiant at the house ever since she started down the lane. She handed the babe to the girl who got up unwillingly. On her way to the door she dragged her feet, hoping that Honey would let up. Once outside she wandered by the windows trying to get a peek inside, hoping to make something of her bad luck. Up and down she went, shifting Honey on one side, then the other.

After a good while the middle door opened and a plain-faced lady with white hair and a cane stood there. It was, Chariter guessed, the Squire's sister. Miss Belle, the valley called her. Hardly ever, they said, did she leave the house. Honey took one look at that strange face and went to screaming again. But the old lady with the cane didn't order them off. She stood there sober and matter of fact. She treated the girl like somebody she had never seen before and never expected to again.

"Isn't she getting heavy for you?" she said without sentiment. "You can bring her in for a while and rest yourself if you care to."

The girl guessed she didn't mind, finding herself in a long room with little furniture, just a straight chair, a painted bench with a back, and some rugs on the floor. This must be, she reckoned, what her mam and Ant Dib called the hall at the Stevenses. Down the line it had doors opening to unknown places on both sides.

"You can wait here," Miss Belle said briefly and the girl let herself down on the plank settee where she tried to hush the babe, lifting her upright against her breast with her face over her shoulder and patting her bottom.

"She'll cam down," she promised.

The old lady's eyes, so dark under her white hair, examined her.

"Mam can't do much with her," the girl explained. "She has to give her to me."

"And what do you do?" Miss Belle asked.

"Oh, I just wrap her up tight and lay her down," Chariter said. "A tight blanket's good for the narves. It makes her feel safe. I heard about it from a woman down at market."

"I'll get you something," Miss Belle offered and came back presently with an old faded blue blanket. Chariter wound it tightly about the child and laid her down beside her on the settee. Almost at once she subsided, and after a few sobs went off to sleep.

The girl looked up to see the dark eyes taking new stock of her.

"Should I know you?" Miss Belle asked.

"I'm Chariter," the girl said and when the old lady looked puzzled, "Dockey Murdoch's my mother."

"Oh, you're a Murdoch," Miss Belle said quickly. Although Chariter looked sharp she couldn't detect anything. She might have said, "Oh, you're a Stevens." Now she paid her the compliment of sitting down, too, taking the straight chair.

"Nice weather we're having," Chariter said to be sociable.

"It's summer. We should have," Miss Belle told her.

"We ain't had much yet," Chariter said. "Granmam looks for rain tomorrow. It had such a heavy dew last night."

"Is that a sign?" the old lady asked.

"She says the farmers 'll have a hard time getting in their hay. Every time they mow it rains."

"I don't think we cut ours yet."

"We don't have much to cut," Chariter said. "Granmam has a stall at market. Maybe you bought from her some time."

"Perhaps I did," Miss Belle said. "It's a long time since I went to market."

"We have the best red raspberries in market, so they say."

"Then I must have," Miss Belle warmed a little. "I love raspberries."

"I like 'em too," Chariter said. "But I don't get much chance to eat any. They fetch thirty cents a box at market."

"I'm sorry," Miss Belle said, "I mean that you don't get to eat many."

They looked at each other and Chariter suddenly felt they had found common ground. She could see less dullness in the sad brown eyes. The talk went better after that. From time to time the girl let her eyes run through the opposite door and into the next room. It must be a mighty big room, she told herself, from the piece she saw of it. In that one piece she could make out a slew of things, peacock feathers in a bowl on a marble top table, the statue of a boy on the mantel, and the gold framed painting of a dog lying on the ground watching chickens. Never had she laid eyes on so many chairs in one corner. The antique dealer behind the market house would go crazy over that table with curved legs, the high painted china lamp on its tall stand and the clock like the one Tom Leck told about, higher than a man, with the moon on its face and striking a tune every now and then.

But what took her eye was the unframed painting of a man in soldier clothes. It set on rails of bamboo fence in the room. When she got a chance, she said something about it.

"Oh, the picture on the easel?" A cruel look came in the old lady's face. "That's Mr. Richard. He died in the service, in Nicaragua, and was buried down there."

Richard, Richard? It was nobody Chariter ever heard of, but she had of a young Dick Goddem. Uncle Nun used to say his name once in a while. Every time she looked back to the picture his eyes seemed to be watching her. Now why would eyes watch her when they belonged to a man she never saw and never would see, for by this time he must be rotted away in that foreign ground?

Miss Belle seemed jogged up by Chariter's notice of the picture.

"His mother kept his room upstairs just as it was when he left," she said. "We've had it that way ever since. Would you like to see it?"

"I don't care," Chariter told her, meaning she would but didn't want to put the old lady to trouble.

Miss Belle rose with her cane. The girl set the back of the old lady's chair against the bench so Honey wouldn't roll off. They climbed the stairs wide enough for three at a time and down a long hall to a room somewhat smaller than the others they passed.

"Nothing in here has been changed since Mr. Richard left," Miss Belle said. "Only the curtains washed. You notice they're almost falling apart. The same sheets and blankets on the bed, the same pictures on the wall and letters on his desk. That's the pen he used. This was his room as a little boy and when he got to be a man he never wanted to change. He said he could always sleep better here."

Chariter stepped slowly into the room. It seemed like going back in time before she was born to a place that had stood still all this while. Her eyes took in everything, the single bed, the pony bridle hanging on the wall, the water jug with a silver stopper standing on a silver tray with a glass and the contraption on the desk that Miss Belle called his typewriter.

"The chimney goes right behind that wall," she said. "It helps keep it warm. And here's the closet where Richard said he saw the devil."

The girl could tell this was something special the way the old lady's eyes sparked. She told how the small boy was bad one day and his mother had put him in the closet. He hollered to be let out. He said the devil was in there. When he came out they asked him if he saw the devil. Yes, he had red hair, the boy said, no clothes on and a black spot on his tail where it got burned in the fire.

Chariter and the old lady had to laugh over that. The girl was in no hurry to leave. She peered at the pictures of girls on the wall. Miss Belle said they were young ladies Mr. Richard used to know. None of them, to Chariter's disappointment, was anybody she knew. When they got back downstairs the rumble of voices from the office had stopped.

"I believe the hearing's over," Miss Belle said, and her cane went across the hall. She came back. "I think your folks have gone."

But when the girl got outside with Honey, her mother was waiting for her up the lane.

"What took you so long?" she scolded, taking the child.

"Miss Belle showed me through the house."

"Well, you needn't a kept her in there all the time," she said, meaning the young one.

Now what made her so cross? the girl wondered.

"How'd Granpap make out?"

"If you'd a stayed out here, you wouldn't have to ask," her mother said. "That old devil's bound him to court trial."

So that's why her mam had her dander up, the girl thought. Or was it? Most times her mother couldn't abide her pap. They were like fighting cocks in the same barnyard. More than once she'd heard her mother say it might do him good if he went to jail a few times. Now why should she get so mad about him just going to court trial? No, there must be something more than that. Chariter looked at her walking sulky beside her. The girl let her that way till they came by the school house.

"You ever hear of the one that got killed in the war? Richard, I think, she said his name was?" she asked though she knew the name well enough.

"Richard? Who's that?" her mam belittled it.

"Richard—in the house back there," the girl told her.

"You mean Dick?" her mam said. She sounded sarcastic. She walked along shutmouthed for a while. "Nun knowed him. They used to go in here together." By in here she meant the school.

"How about you?" Chariter persisted.

"What about me?" she came back touchy.

"You know what I asked you."

Dockey walked a while.

"Yes, I knowed him. We all knowed him."

"What did you know about him?"

"Why should I know anything special about him?"

"Well, if you all knew him you must a known something."

"I know he used to drink heavy. Most of the Goddems done that. He started in young. He never done it at home on account of his pap. He'd drive to Tinsburg and stop at our place to sober up on the way home. His horse would a took him home drunk or sober but his old man would have give him jesse, so he come in at our place."

"How good did you know him?" the girl asked.

"Good enough," she said shortly.

"Where was I when he went to war?"

"Who, Dick? How should I know?" It sounded careful to the girl.

"Well, where was he when I was born? Around here or some place else?"

"I just told you I don't know." Her voice had raised.

"You'd know if he was living or dead," the girl came back at her. She wouldn't be put off now.

"How kin I mind back that far?" her mother stood

her off. "Why should I a kep track of him? Maybe I was carrying you when I heard of it. Maybe I had you already. I don't know."

"When you heard what?"

"That he'd run off some place and joined up. It was no war."

Something went over the girl when she heard that. So he had run off? What was it, she wondered, he had run off from?

"Had he red hair?" she put to her.

"No, he hadn't," her mam said shortly. "And he wasn't dark complected and he wasn't light." She turned her face toward the girl and her eyes fastened on her like bright razors. "Now don't you go getting any notions. You're just common folks like the rest of us. Don't try to fool yourself with hifalutin idees."

CHAPTER X

THIS was July and so far Fulliam had carried out what he said. All June Chariter never laid eyes on him. She knew he still worked for his Uncle Fulliam and that he came home once in a while, for Babe said he saw him up the valley, and Heb, too. That's all they did say and she didn't ask for more. Oh, she could spell out what Fulliam was up to. If he didn't come buzzing for honey around her, he must be getting it some place else. Either that or he wanted her to think so, she didn't know for certain which, only that he was a die-hard and it had no dodge he wouldn't resort to if he reckoned it would make her come around.

Others soon took notice.

"What's up between you and Fulliam?" her mam wanted to know.

"If anything's up, it's on his side, not mine," Chariter told her.

"Why don't he come around any more?" her mother persisted.

"If he don't come," Chariter said, "somebody else will."

And that's the way it worked out, but not like she reckoned.

July started mild enough. The day after the Fourth, Harrison Laird drove up the lane in the Goddem's pickup truck. He wanted to see Ant Dib. They were out on the barn floor shaking old straw out of the bed ticks and stuffing in new. The old was mostly hard dust from laying and turning on it all winter. The new had come fresh, bright and good-smelling out of the harvest field. It was a holy terror to lie on the first couple of weeks, scratchy as a hog's back. Here and yon it jagged through the tick. Till it got broke down right by the boys, Chariter would sooner sleep on the floor. For the first month or so Heb and Nun slept with their clothes on.

You could tell Harrison Laird was the Squire's farmer, a hickory sprout of a man, upstanding, not scared to look you in the eye. He got right down to business with Dib.

"Miss Belle has to go to the hospital and she wondered if you could come and help out when she comes home."

You could see Ant Dib and Granmam itched to ask the matter with the old lady.

"You mean by day or all the time?" Ant Dib wanted to know.

"Well," Harrison said, "I guess she'll need somebody all the time till she can take hold herself again. My wife can get meals for the Squire and clean the place while she's off, but she can't be over night and day with her young ones at home."

"I got young ones at home myself," Ant Dib pointed out.

"We thought maybe your mam and the girl here could take care of them like they do Dockey's," Harrison said. "You wouldn't have to work all the time, just so you'd be there when she needs you."

Ant Dib shook her head.

"I don't have to work all the time here. I have a man who earns a living for me. He don't like for me to work out."

Harrison Laird looked disappointed.

"Well, if that's the way you feel about it," he said and turned away.

"I can come, if you want me to!" Chariter called out.

Harrison Laird turned to look at her. The girl read mistrust in his eyes.

"I'm stout," she told him. "I can do most everything she can, can't I, Ant Dib?"

Ant Dib didn't know as she liked that, admitting a girl was good as she was.

"They don't want a young one like you," she said roughly.

"I was sixteen last month," Chariter told Harrison Laird. "You can tell Miss Belle. She knows me. Tell her it's the one that wrapped the baby to sleep."

Harrison didn't say he would and didn't say he wouldn't but Dockey said plenty when she came home.

"You're not going to live with them people," she laid down the law. "Besides, Granmam needs you here."

"I ain't helpless yet," Granmam told her tartly. "And you don't need to make such a fuss. They ain't asked her yet."

The Murdochs never knew if Harrison Laird had gone any other place or not but he stopped back in a couple of days. The girl could come, he told Granmam. The squire was taking the old lady to the hospital tomorrow. When she got back, they'd let the girl know. Then she could bring her traps and stay a while.

The news that Chariter Murdoch had hired out to the Goddems went in a short time over the valley. Now wouldn't you expect most folks to be glad a girl had gumption to make some wages for herself? But not those three old men. Tom Leck, Uncle Nun reported, had nothing for it. Neither had Nobe Gandy. And Granpap was fit to be tied when he found out. He and Nobe were out in the Murdoch oak grove Sunday afternoon raising sand over it with Vince Foote and the others.

"I don't blame her working out some place if she wants," Nobe declared. "I knowed plenty done it at her age. But what does she have to go to him for?"

"Don't look at me!" Dockey said angrily. "I didn't say she could."

"No, but what would she want to go to the God-dems for?" Nobe demanded. "Them people are nothing to her." He looked around as if daring them to say different.

Granpap kicked off a shoe to scratch his foot.

"You'd think somebody would tell me," he complained. "They told everybody else before her granpap. Even that new mailman. I had to hear it from somebody not even related."

"We didn't tell you on purpose," Ant Dib said sharply. "We didn't want you bellyaching she couldn't go when she didn't know herself if they wanted her."

"You didn't tell me," Granpap shook his finger at her, "because you know'd I'd a put my foot down on it."

"You'd a had nothing to do with it one way or another," Ant Dib said.

"Now my own granchild," Granpap told Nobe bitterly, "is hired out to the black hound that bound me to court. And for something I never did and never even had in my head." He looked around for confirmation.

"I never done much of anything either the time he got me," Nobe said. "I wouldn't of minded the fine so much but he had to give me a long lecture on trapping out of season. Mind you, it was only the day before." Nobe had started to shout. "Not twenty four hours before the rightful and lawful season opened. And for that I had to pay ten dollars and listen to him tell me off. Any man can make a mistake on the day of the month, I told him. A man shouldn't be fined for looking at the calendar wrong. But he wouldn't hear to it. He said it had no excuse for breaking the law. I could hardly hold back telling what I thought of him but I was too smart. I kep my mouth shut. He just wanted me to blackguard him so he could double my fine. All I done was look at him. He knew what was in my mind. But he couldn't fine me for thinking, could he? I come out best over him that time."

"There's none of the Goddems any good," Granpap said.

"Old Dick wasn't so bad," Uncle Nun put in.

"He never done anything for me," Nobe said.

"He wasn't like the squire," Uncle Nun grinned. "I mind when him and his wife lived in that big house in Tinsburg where Doc Noble lives now. I was only a boy but I seen him more'n once. He liked to put on old clothes and work out in his garden. They said he had flowers and bushes from half way around the world. He kep it like a show place and one time when all the flowers were out a lady from Hagerstown or some place come by in her machine. She had her driver stop so she could look in. She seen old Dick digging in his old clothes and took him for the gardener. She told him how nice he kep the place and if he ever wanted a better job he should come see her in Hagerstown. What wages he was getting, she'd pay more. Old Dick never told who he was. No, he looked down on the ground and said, 'Well, lady, it's not the wages. I have special privileges here.' 'What privileges is that?' she said. 'Well,' he told her, 'I kin sleep with the lady of the house.' " Uncle Nun slapped his leg. "That's what old Dick told her. Jerry Korner was out at his place and heard him. 'I have special privileges here,' he said, 'I kin sleep with the lady of the house.' "

A painful smile went around the circle.

"Maybe old Dick wasn't so bad but he was the only one," Nobe said grudgingly.

"I never could go any of them." Granpap made a face. "Maybe not the first Goddem here in the valley. He was all man, my granpap used to say. If you said or done what you oughtn'ter, he'd knock you down or string you up. He owned the whole valley them days and anybody wanted to live here had to make a covenant with him. His word was law, Granpap said. Folks looked up to him, were scared of him. If you was in his favor, he'd do most anything for you. But if he didn't like you or you done him wrong, he'd make your life hell."

Granpap halted to look around at his hearers. Then he went on drawing his breath through the corners of his mouth in scorn.

"But this here Minor Goddem! Who does he figger he is? Most of his land is gone. Half the people have no use for him. Nobody has the fear of a Goddem any more. And yet he goes around lording it over us what we kin do and kain't, sending us to court if we don't do his bidding."

Chariter heard them curiously. Now why did they have it in so hard for the Goddems? And who would have thought that Fulliam would throw in with them? Even if his father and the squire had had trouble one time over borrowed money that was in no hurry to be paid back? Not that she saw Fulliam lately, neither last Sunday or this, only the next. He sent Fox to say he had something to tell her. If she wanted to hear it she better be at the school house after Sunday dinner. It was on the tip of her tongue to say that if he wanted to see her he knew where to find her. But then, she recollected, she might never know what was in his mind, for that would gall Fulliam. So she swallowed her pride and went. No Fulliam in sight when she got there but after while he showed up from behind the school. He cut a figure in his town hat and clothes.

"What's this about you going to be maid at the God-dems?" he put to her.

So that was it? she said to herself. It rose in her to answer back, what if I am and what is it to you? She looked at him standing there close to her, handsome, ready to eat fire and something in her melted.

"I guess it's so, if that's what you mean," she said meek enough.

"I don't like it," he told her angrily. "I don't want you working out for anybody."

She looked at him. What did he mean by such talk after giving her the go-by?

"I work for Mam and Granmam and Ant Dib all the time," she said mildly. "I done it ever since I'm big enough to reach in a wash tub."

"That's at home," he pointed out. "I don't care what you do at home but you don't work out for anybody else if you look to live with me."

It was on the tip of her tongue to say, I thought you told me never to look for living with you, that you made out to live with that Maybel?

"If I lived with you, Fulliam," she said, "I'd have to work just the same."

"Yes, but you wouldn't be working out," he told her.

"You wouldn't have to eat in some other man's kitchen or do lackey work for him."

Chariter let her eyes rest on him. That was Fulliam, thin skinned and touchy, contrary as all get out, throw him in the river and he'd float upstream, raising the roof over some piddling hurt to his pride. Oh, he would let her slave for him for nothing and for his four, five or six young ones besides and all of them eat in his or Granmam's kitchen three times a day, for they would have had no special room to eat in like the Stevenses or the Goddems, and Fulliam would think nothing of it. But let her go out and try to make some wages cooking for the squire; and she might as well lay out with some strange man.

"I can't go back on my word now," she told him. "I can't say one time I'm coming and another time I'm backing out. And her in the hospital with no woman in the house to come home to."

Oh, she knew how Fulliam would take to that. Once he took a stand, he didn't like to back down. He argued all the way down the road and when he left told her not to expect him to go half way toward making up with her again.

Now wasn't it curious that Granpap said something much the same at home?

"Once you hire out to that shyster, don't look for me to come up and see you."

"I guess that won't make her mad," Granmam told him.

"I'll come, Chariter," Babe said in a low voice, keeping his eyes off Granpap.

"No, you won't," Granmam said sharply. "You have no business up there and you kin stay away till you do."

The weeks went deeper into summer till Chariter had her job. Some times she wondered had she spoken too quick. Not that it mattered about Fulliam. He hadn't been coming around anyhow. But her own family acted strange to her, even Uncle Nun and Heb. Only Granmam was the same, a little sharp some times, but then she always was, even handed, keeping the fair weather side out most of the time, acting like she was pleased over some secret matter she never had been before.

"Now mind you put your best foot forward up there," she instructed. "Remember we're not like some town bodies who don't care how they act at the table. We don't eat with our forks and then stick them in the pot with everybody else's. Forks are for spearing bread, meat and potatoes. The knife's the proper tool to eat with."

"The Stevenses use a butter knife," Ant Dib mentioned.

"What's the use of a knife just for butter," Granmam asked, "unless you eat with your knife?"

"We don't have one," Fox said.

"We don't need any. We wipe our knives on our bread before reaching in the butter. And you better not let me catch you shirking."

"How do they hold stuff on a fork?" Babe wanted to know. "You'd think it would run through."

"And keep in mind, girl," Granmam went on, "the place to drink your coffee from. Pour it out nice and cool in the saucer. It don't look so hoggish as swilling it out of a cup."

"You kaint blow coffee cool in a cup," Fox told her.

"If they's one thing shiftless," Granmam went on again, "it's drying dishes with a rag that wasn't wrung out in the dishpan first. A dry rag don't wipe soap and dried eggs off your dishes. And no double spreading! If you want apple butter on your bread, you don't need butter, and if you want butter, you don't need apple butter."

Chariter felt grateful when Ant Dib took a hand. It showed that she wasn't against her for going up to the Goddems.

"I wouldn't do more'n you have to, Chariter," she advised. "When I was up at the Stevenses I always kep in mind the story about Barnaby Bill. You know he went horseback to the mill with a sack of wheat on his shoulder. 'What did he do that for?' Uncle Robby asked him. Barnaby said that sack of wheat was too heavy for his old mare."

"I know you won't shame us, Chariter," Granmam concluded. "We brought you up right. You know to wipe the gravy off your plate with a piece of bread before you turn the clean side up for pie. And when you eat corn, you want to let the squire and old lady pull the string through their teeth first. They might not like using the corn string after you."

"Chariter," Ant Dib mentioned, "maybe you could get me some slips from Miss Belle's house trees? I mean the ones she keeps in tubs the year round."

"I think," Granmam said, "one kind she calls Holy Gander and the other Nabisco."

So it went, first one, then the other. The girl nodded gravely. Three heads, she reckoned, were better than one, if one was a cabbage head as Uncle Nun used to say. She'd take all the advice she could get beforehand, but once she got there she would use her own head. That's why she had one. It just made her feel good to have both Ant Dib and Granmam looking after her.

All the same she had a sinking feeling when Harrison Laird stopped to say Miss Belle was coming home tomorrow. Her own home place never looked so good as it did next morning when she started down the lane. Fox and Babe said they'd go along and carry her traps but Granmam put a stop to that.

"The squire didn't hire you," she said. "You kin stay home."

The Grandfathers

All the way up the road those she saw working in their fields looked good to the girl. They didn't have to go off from their home place to earn a living. But then, she consoled herself, you had to make a break some time. When you got married you had to cut yourself off from your mam and granmam and start a new homestead. She might as well get used to it now. Then it wouldn't go so hard next time. Just the same the long Goddem lane that had looked handsome to her the other time was like the road to the graveyard when she went down it today. She had to knock three times on the back door.

"Oh, it's you," the squire said and let her in. The kitchen was dark and shut in with strange smells and unfamiliar fixens.

Only when she saw the old lady did she come to herself. The squire told her how to go up. She pushed gingerly in the room to make sure she was getting in the right place and not to somebody washing all over in a fine flowered crockery wash basin on the floor. The girl hardly knew Miss Belle propped up in her bed. She hadn't expected to see the face on those piled up pillows so eaten and gray. The eyes were mostly sockets and the boney hands on the white coverlet had dark raised-up veins. Why, a broom under the covers would have made more body than the old lady's breasts and hams.

"I'm so glad you could come. Charity, is it?" she said and gave her a faint smile.

"Yes'm, I'm here," the girl said quickly, not too sad or homesick any more. The sight of that face and body had cured her. She could be of plenty use here, she reckoned. She needn't feel sorry for herself any more.

CHAPTER XI

NOBODY ever told Chariter she had second sight like Carrie Taylor who once lived up in the woods where the bootlegger lived now. The girl reckoned she didn't need it to see what lay ahead for Miss Belle. The old lady could hardly get out on the floor save when she had to, but always was she master patient about it. You'd reckon she'd never done more than lay in bed all her life and got used to it. Or else inside of her she'd given up and not told anybody yet.

Chariter did her best to jack up her hopes.

"Lots of sick folks get well and stout again," she told her. "Granmam knew a woman in market never been well a day in her life till she got run over by a truck and twenty two bones broken. After that she limped a little but said she felt better than she ever did before."

Miss Belle smiled faintly. The girl went on.

"You daresen't give up. A man in Jeffs Valley had

blood poison in his thumb. They told him to stick it in a tomato and keep it there night and day. Uncle Nun said it was a little unhandy going to bed and cutting his meat at the table. His woman complained it ran over the floor and bed clothes. But it done the job."

The patient's eyes twinkled.

"I wish I had just blood poisoning in my thumb, Charity," she said. "We'd surely try it."

"You got to do more'n try," the girl told her. "Granpap knew a man had a sore foot. He could have cured it with fresh cow manure poultice, but do you think he would? No, he said he wasn't going to walk after no cow waiting for his salve. The sore went up his leg and would have killed him. They had to take it off."

Miss Belle actually laughed.

"You're good for the soul, Charity," she said.

Most always when she talked to her a while, the girl could see blood come up in the drained cheeks but it never lasted. The squire had set a fine brass handbell on his sister's bed to call her. That bell, Miss Belle said, had rung for dinner a hundred years ago. But almost never did the old lady ring it. The house stayed so quiet upstairs the girl working downstairs would stop and cock her head to listen. She'd reckon she'd better run up to see if Miss Belle wanted anything. The old lady usually did but seldom was the bell touched.

"I knew you'd be in looking after me soon," she'd say.

The girl ran those back steps nigh onto fifty times a day, and every day she thought those tired old eyes looked at her a little further away than yesterday. Oh, there was something in this big house besides her, the old lady and the squire, and that thing was Death. Chariter never saw it but late afternoons she could feel it on the dark back stairs when she passed, and she could, too, in the upstairs bedrooms where it likely had been on business many times before. The furniture in those dim rooms stood around like great wooden beasts. The high carved headboards of the bed looked down on her. The heavy curtains minded her of shrouds. She shook a curtain once half looking for the Death thing to fly out, but all that came out was dust like from an old grave.

"I reckon I'll let the dust in after this," she told herself.

The place upstairs that felt nearest to home was the room that had been Dick Goddem's, the Dick her mam and Uncle Nun knew. Maybe Death had never come in here but had to find him down somewheres a thousand miles or more. She could feel the difference from the rest of the house the minute she stepped in. You could tell the person that slept in that half bed wasn't some old graybeard like in those other rooms. No, he had been young and full of sap like her, enjoying life, not ready to give up for the graveyard. Most everything in here, even those pictures of strange girls on the wall, hit it off with her, went with the grain. It felt good to have her own room close behind. Sometimes after leaving Miss Belle for the night, she came in here and laid back in Dick Goddem's Morris chair, letting the door stand open for light.

She only wished they had a lock of Dick Goddem's hair like they had of other Goddems, some behind a pane of glass on the wall or setting in a little frame on a bureau. Miss Belle told her whose hair they were. They had all come to their ends in this house or close by so it was easy to snip at their heads when they lay in their bed or coffin. Now Dick Goddem had laid dead too far away for a pair of his Ant Belle's shears to go snipping at him. It was a pity. A lock of hair fetched the dead closer than anything else, closer still than a picture or letter. Hold it with your fingers and you could see right in front of you the face that went with that hair.

The dead that had gone out of this old house seemed mighty close once summer was done. The first leaves of the shumack and sour gum she knew had already turned color along the crick. Soon Fox and Babe and Ant Dib and Granmam would be gathering red and "yaller" maple leaves for the cow stable. She wished she could see them all again but she couldn't look for them to come up here. No, it was up to her to go down to see them. But Miss Belle was too sick to ask for a half day off now.

"The doctor thinks somebody should sleep in the next room to her," the squire told Chariter. "And keep the door open."

"Yes, sir," the girl said. She knew that somebody was her. She never liked that next room. That's where she had shaken the curtain looking for Death to fly out. Bed, bureau and washstand were black walnut carved like coffins and so all-fired heavy she could hardly move them to clean. She didn't sleep much in that bed. They kept a lamp lit all night in the sick room. The half light that came through her door made fearsome bodies and faces out of the old furniture. Sometimes she had the feeling those ancient pieces talked to each other.

"Shut up!" she'd make faces at them. "You're only dead wood. You can't talk."

What troubled her worse than the bed "suit" in here was the clock in Miss Belle's room. It was a fine polished wooden piece with a steeple at the top and it struck in a terrible hurry. You heard it all over the house, though Miss Belle said she seldom noticed it, so used to the sound she was. But the girl hated to hear Miss Belle's hours gobbled up so fast. She hated still worse the busy-body minute hand. She couldn't see it from where she lay but she could hear it counting off the seconds of Miss

Belle's life from which there was no reprieve. And no pity either. It was the hand of doom going around, that's what it was. It gave the girl silent despair for her charge and patron. A picture downstairs told how mighty pretty she had been. It showed a young girl with thick brown hair sitting side saddle on a fine horse with friends on other horses close around her. Now she lay old and alone in her bed with her pitiful thin white hair.

"I'm just glad eyes don't turn white and drop out," Chariter told herself, for Miss Belle still had the softest brown eyes you ever wanted to look in. They were eyes like those of the praying angel on the wall over the sick woman's head.

Now wouldn't you guess that the praying angel would be wrong and that bossy minute hand on the clock right! Mrs. Laird stayed over a few nights so Chariter could get some rest back in her own room. Toward the last a nurse in white came from Dumont to stay around the clock. Chariter was only too glad to cook for her and redd up her room just so Miss Belle had somebody with her all the time. The old lady didn't want to eat. She didn't even want water.

"It doesn't taste good any more," she whispered.

It fetched back to Chariter's mind what Granmam told her of the time Granmam's own mam lay dying over in Porter Valley. The old woman said she wished she had a drink of water from the spring at home. Granmam had taken a lantern and tramped a mile through the mountains to fetch back a kettle of water from that home spring. Gladly now would Chariter do the same, but it had no special water the old maiden lady thirsted for. Not even on the fateful night the clock struck four times for the mortal hour when most folks, they say, depart from this world.

"It's a mercy," Mrs. Laird told the nurse when she came over. "She's out of her suffering now and can rest."

The girl said nothing. Maybe Mrs. Laird and the nurse could rest better but not Chariter Murdoch. She had lost a friend. Nobody knew that better than her. Not that she had time to think much about it. If she had work before, she had double and triple now, busy from six in the morning till eleven at night with people traipsing in, cousins from far away places to stay in the house and be fed and cleaned up after. The undertaker made his calls, not Fulliam or his uncle from Earlville but strangers from Dumont with a machine hearse like Fulliam always said he wanted so a funeral wouldn't take all day. Chariter had no chance to get to the cemetery. All she could do was stand in her apron in the back hall and listen to the Episcopal preacher in his robes say seemly things about Miss Belle. Soon as they left for the cemetery, she and Mrs. Laird got busy with the dinner for them who would come back for it.

Already that night it seemed empty in the house with Miss Belle off in her grave and twice as much next day when the folks from other places had gone. Chariter reckoned she would soon be gone, too. She made what noise she could cleaning up just for company to herself. She wanted to hear some life around the place. The first supper she fetched in the dining room for the squire she expected him to turn her out. But not a word to her. She told herself he had talked through Harrison Laird for her to come and she reckoned he would talk through him for her to go.

And that's the way it worked out. Harrison Laird came to the kitchen from the office.

"I just saw the squire," he said. "He told me Miss Belle talked to him about you. She said she wished he could keep you on after she died."

A warm feeling ran over the girl. So the old lady had been her intercessor. But she better not feel too good about it. She hadn't heard the whole story yet. Harrison Laird had something more in his eyes. He went on.

"The squire said he didn't know as he could do what Miss Belle said. I told him I thought you wouldn't mind. I said I guessed it was pretty lonesome for a young girl here all alone and you'd be ready to quit and go home."

Chariter stood there.

"Why did the squire say he couldn't do it?"

"Well, he said he didn't like the idea of living alone in the house with a young girl. It might make talk in the valley."

The first thing the girl felt was anger, not so much at Harrison Laird for saying it but at the old man for thinking such a thing. So he was afraid of having a Murdoch woman alone in the house with him? Well, he needn't be. Let him come around her room at night and he'd get his whiskers yanked out. What for notions went on in his mind anyway? What kind of talk was that from somebody who might be your own granpappy for all you knew? She couldn't say for certain since her own mam claimed she didn't know.

"If Miss Belle wanted me to stay, I'll stay," Chariter informed Harrison stoutly. "You can tell him he don't need to mind me since it might be we're related."

Harrison Laird could keep his face pretty straight, but she thought something ran under his tanned hide when she said that. How much he told the squire she never knew, only that he gave her mighty sharp looks next day when she served him his meals in the dining room and on the following day when he sat down with her for a cup of coffee in the kitchen. Oh, he wasn't over friendly or familiar. It seemed he just wanted a chance to look her over. He never changed the high-minded way he always acted. It was a trick, she reckoned, that must have come down a long way in the blood of them that had land a plenty in the family and were used to telling other folks what they could do and what they couldn't. Now a Murdoch had no line of bluebloods in his veins to set him above common folks. No, she could feel the Murdoch part flinching inside of her when he told her to sit down and have some coffee with him. Oh, he talked to her nice enough but just the way he did it in the back of his Goddem mouth like he had a cold potato in it took away her comfort. She reckoned she knew now why her Granpappy Murdoch went to hollering when he blackguarded the squire. It was to cut him down to his own size.

Oh, if she wanted to, she could tell Harrison Laird and the squire that living up here wasn't all she had cracked it up to be. The house was like one of those tombs over in Africy she'd read about in her school geography. Likely it had been to Dick Goddem, too, and that's why he came so often to the Murdochs. Their place wasn't grand but it had life there. She wished she could see it right now with onions drying on newspaper spread over the front room floor, with Granmam and Ant Dib standing at the kitchen stove, Uncle Nun and Heb washing up, the heavy thick white plates and big loaf already on the table where forks would soon be reaching for the thick slices as they fell. The young ones would be rutching on their bench, and Babe running to tell Granpap to come down.

Now wasn't it a pity that her half day off didn't come till next week? With Miss Belle so sick and the nurse to run lackey for, she hadn't been home for such a long time. Then she heard something at the kitchen door, a kind of scratching or the wind blowing sleet. She opened it and there stood Babe in scuffed shoes and a coat that had been Heb's and Fox's before him. She could have hugged and kissed the little feller. Babe said he'd been up to the bootlegger for Granpap and thought he'd stop and see if she was all right. Never had that thin little feller looked so good to her. Oh, she could tell now if she hadn't before that they were of the same Murdoch blood, and him her favorite if she had any. Not that she dare make much fuss over him. She daresn't give away that she pined for home.

"Well, come in," she said hearty like to a grownup. "You're a sight for sore eyes."

Babe stepped in the squire's kitchen gingerly, looking around as if half afraid the boogy man would jump out at him. She had to coax the coat and cap off him, to get him down on a chair at the stove. Such a good feeling went over her to see him sitting there.

"Everything all right at home?" she asked, for she knew he must have come against Granmam's orders.

"Jess's got a tooth," he said. "Jessie don't have none yet."

Chariter smiled her pleasure. If it had nothing worse

than that at home, she had no cause for misgiving. Babe sat there watching her mighty close.

"You going to live here now, Chariter?" and when she nodded. "You know what they say about you?"

It gave her a turn. She almost said, "What?" mighty sharp, but spoke something else instead.

"Who's they?" she wanted to know.

"Pete Barrow. He says a man come over Black Log Mountain in a big machine with red wheels and a tire hanging over the back. He said, did Pete know a girl by the name of Chariter Murdoch living in this valley. He said he just wished he was lucky as her."

"Well, I don't know as I'd swallow everything Pete Barrow said," Chariter told him.

"You know that woman has a stall next to Granmam's?" Babe went on. "Granmam said an old darkey asked her why don't that girl that used to come with Mrs. Murdoch come any more? I tell you, the old darkey said, something good's a coming to her."

Chariter looked at him.

"Folks like to talk, Babe," she said. "What did Granmam say?"

"She told Uncle Nun it was soft sodder."

"What did Uncle Nun say?"

"He said hogs kin see the wind when folks kain't. Aren't you scared all alone with him in the house?"

"Who?"

"The squire and all them bones of folks he killed and hid in the cellar?"

"Bosh and moonshine!" she said. "Folks made that up to get even with him for giving judgement against them."

"Don't he growl and snap at you sometimes?"

"No, he don't. He talks to me like anybody else. He even comes out in the kitchen and sits down sometimes like you are now."

"What does he say?"

"Lots of things. He asked me if Babe was your real name and the same about Fox. He wanted to know if you were baptized. I told him I never was either."

"What did you say my name was?"

"I told him it was Lancelot Gerald Murdoch. He wanted to know where we got the name, Fox. I told him when he was little he looked like a little old he-fox peeking out of his den."

"Did he put our names down in his book?"

"What book?"

"Why, they say he keeps a big book like God Almighty. Everything anybody does in the valley he puts down in that book."

"Only if they get in trouble," Chariter said. "If you want your name in that book, just go and steal a sheep or rob the Tinsburg bank."

"I don't want my name in," Babe said. He was silent

a while. "Kin he still put his pants on standing up or must he sit down like Granpappy?"

"What are you talking about, Babe Murdoch!" she flared at him. "How should I know! Who put you up to saying that? You been talking to Fulliam?"

"I seen him but he didn't say nothing. I just wondered my own self last night in bed."

He jumped up when a door shut somewhere in the house. There was no way but that he put on his coat and cap, and pick up Granpap's bottle of mule.

"Granmam said she'd britch me if I come around," he begged. "You won't tell her?"

Long after he had gone she could still feel the little feller sitting there, could smell the good home smell of wood smoke, ham, fried potatoes and other Murdoch standbys coming from where he sat. She reckoned she must have been homesick and still was, but felt glad she hadn't given herself away.

Anyhow that's what she thought. It spited her that she was wrong. She must have dropped something or else Babe could spell out more than she gave him credit for. Saturday night came a tapping on the kitchen door and when she opened it, there stood Ant Dib and Granmam with the twins.

"Babe said he seen you up the lane when he went by in the road and you looked peaked," Granmam made excuse for coming.

Oh, that sharp-eyed young deceiver of a Babe, the girl thought. She hadn't reckoned how much he had seen or put together.

"So we guessed we'd surprise you," Ant Dib said.

Now who would have looked for such luck tonight? she told herself. Her own flesh and blood here in the kitchen for company on the long evening. She had to see Jess's tooth and feel with her finger in Jessie's mouth if she couldn't find signs of one breaking through. She held first one then the other, all the time talking of things she knew Granmam and Ant Dib wanted to know about, like Miss Belle's sickness, dying and funeral, what they had for funeral dinner, how good was Mrs. Laird's cooking and what kind of snitz and mince pies she made.

When at last they said they had to go, she asked didn't they want to see where she slept? which she knew they did, and the rest of the house besides if it could be managed, so she took them up the back stairs and showed them her own room with its cracked marbletop mahogany bureau where she kept her traps, and after that Dick Goddem's room next to it, pointing out how everything was kept all these years like it used to be, showing off the corner closet where he claimed as a little feller he had seen the devil. Jess was sleepy and fretful and Ant Dib made to put him in the closet which set him off to kicking and screaming. It made them laugh at the little monkey. By hokey day it was good to hear them all, babes and grownups, putting life into this dead old house.

Coming down Chariter fetched them the front way, first the upstairs hall so they could look in the room where Miss Belle died, expecting after that to show the front of the house downstairs, for the squire kept mostly to his office he called the library. But when they started down the main stairs there was the old man standing at the bottom looking up to find out where all the racket came from. Granmam and Ant Dib shut up like clams and even Jess swallowed his bawling. Chariter reckoned maybe she had gone too far showing the house but she wouldn't give in now.

"This is my granmam and Ant Dib and her twinnies," she made them acquainted with the squire like she had heard during Miss Belle's funeral.

The squire stood like a fierce statue, inclining his head a little. Granmam and Ant Dib gave him no more than he did. They couldn't get away from there quick enough. Only when they were safe back in the kitchen did they look and act natural.

"Now we got to go for sure," Granmam said.

"You don't know how nice it was for you to come," Chariter told them. "Maybe now Mam will too."

Ant Dib and Granmam gave each other a look.

"You know your mam," Granmam said. "I wouldn't look for her or your granpap up here."

"I know why he won't come," the girl said. "But not why she won't."

"Well, you kin talk to her your own self."

"I did try to going home from the hearing. She wouldn't say nothing."

"She don't say much to me either," Granmam told shortly.

"You could tell her I'd show her the house and Dick Goddem's room," Chariter promised.

"I guess she don't want to see his room or the house either," Granmam said.

When they had gone the girl recollected that not a word on either side had been spoken about Fulliam.

Next week on her half day off, Chariter went home and up the Stevens lane to wait. She had a chore shooing back the young ones who wanted to tag after. She felt it was worth it when she saw the look her mother gave her as she came along.

"What you doing over here?" she said first thing. The girl stood her ground.

"I have a crow to pick with you, Mam. Why don't you come to see me some time?"

"I have plenty more to do than run after you," her mother said tartly. "Somebody has to keep Honey."

"Fox or Uncle Nun or Chick could do that."

"And what if I have somebody visiting me? Am I to let him set and run off to see you?"

"You could come some other time then?"

"Maybe I could but I ain't a going to," her mam informed her.

"Are you mad at me?" the girl wondered.

"No, I'm not mad at you any more than I always was."

"Are you mad at somebody?" Chariter persisted.

The other stayed silent and the girl, too, till they got to the second turn. Then her mam spoke.

"I kin see you any time you come home."

"Why don't you want to come up to the house? You went to the hearing," Chariter said.

"You kin be up there if you like," her mam told her bitterly. "I kain't."

For a moment the girl had a flash of light. Moments afterward she could still see, or thought she could, a glimmer of how her mother felt and why. She remembered what her granmam had once told her, that hardly would Chariter have known her mam as a young girl, so sociable and lively she was, and pretty as a picture. It gave Chariter a turn to think of her then and how she was now, but that, she reckoned, was the way life ran. Never could a body go back and make things like they were. All the way to the bridge the hard footsteps sounded beside her. At the first plank her mother turned with something working on her face, taking up the talk where they had left off, farther back.

"Even if I could a come I wouldn't of last Saturday night and let that old devil treat me like he did Dib and Mam."

"He didn't treat them bad," Chariter protested. "He didn't say nothing."

"They told me what he done," her mam said angrily. "He stood there like his place was too good for a Murdoch to walk in. Well, you kin have him. If he's the granpap you want, he's the one you're a going to have. And you kin tell the old buzzard I said so."

A flood of feeling for her mam rushed over the girl. She had to fight it all the way to the road and up the Murdoch lane. The dam had broken at last, the word had been spoken, or at least as much as it likely ever would. Coming into her Granmam Murdoch's house she felt almost a stranger and less one when she took the key from under the Goddem back step that night. Oh, she had too much sense to figure it would make much difference to the squire but it did to her. Not a word more would she say unless she had to, even if he sat down and ate his breakfast with her.

She wasn't born yesterday. It didn't take her mam to tell her that life wasn't all it was cracked up to be. She minded a piece in her school reader about a rich

man in Old England who told his daughter never to
darken his door again. But when she died and the old
man found he had a grandchild, he couldn't rest till
he sent for that girl of his own flesh and blood. He took
her into his house, gave her fine dresses to wear and a
coach to ride in. This is my granddaughter, he told
everybody. But that was storybook stuff. Somebody
had made it up. It would never happen in real life, least-
wise not around here. That Bailer girl in Jeffs Valley
knew who her pap was, and him a neighbor old enough
to be her granpap. She started as a little girl going over
to see him and his sister and got to staying with them,
but never a word between them about who he was. No,
she called him Billy like everybody else, and when he
said, "your pap" he didn't mean himself but her mam's
pap, for she had uncles and ants her own age she grew
up with. And that, Chariter reckoned, was the way it
would be here. How could it be any way else? The
whole valley knew how it was. Her mam knew how it
was and she herself guessed she knew now. For whose
benefit would the squire have to make it any different?

No, she reckoned, that's the way life ran and that's
the way it would stay.

CHAPTER XII

THAT winter without Fulliam went better than Chariter had looked for. Likely it went well enough for him, too. Men reckoned themselves so much in the world, something special, hard to do without and sure to make life sour if they left you. Where he spent his off time now, who he hung around with and what foolish woman he bragged to and bent to his will she didn't know, but if he guessed she rocked the winter away here in this kitchen pining for him or that she laid in her bed at night wetting her pillow with grieving, he had another guess coming. If he could make out without her, she could without him, and she didn't give a hait what his Maybel or some other soft headed woman looked like. She knew well enough what such would look like a couple or more years from now.

As for herself, she still had a good time out of life. Dib and Granmam and the boys came to see her. She hardly missed a week going home. Christmas day Tom Leck pulled his case against Granpappy out of court, saying he guessed Culy hadn't fired his barn after all. Of course, he did it only for Granmam and the rest and all the meals he ate at the Murdochs. After the new year, Granmam took Chariter along to market to buy some clothes and shoes for herself at the place next to the fish store.

Fulliam could live his own life, she reckoned, and she would hers. She might have known, she told herself afterward, that sooner or later she'd have to eat her words. First it was Fox who came in to see her on his way back from Nicodemus for Uncle Nun. He stood his quart and pop bottle of mule on the kitchen table.

They had a nice little visit till Chariter's eyes rested on those two bottles.

"How come Uncle Nun gets some extra?" she wondered.

"Oh, that pop bottle ain't for him. It's for me from Nicodemus," Fox said.

Chariter's face darkened.

"Does Mam and Granmam know what he gives you?"

"What they don't know don't hurt them," Fox said.

"Well, he's giving you no more," Chariter told him.

"It don't hurt me none," Fox protested. "Just makes me feel good. He gives Babe a pop bottle, too."

"I never saw it."

"He never brung it in. He hides it up the lane like I do mostly. He said he drank some last time after coming out from seeing you and he could run home like a deer. Only he fell on a rock and busted the pop bottle."

"Served him right," Chariter said. "He's going to run home like a deer no more. Nor you either."

"You're not going to take my mule?" Fox said alarmed.

"No, I'm not but you're going to tell Nicodemus that if he ever gives you or Babe another pop bottle of that stuff I'm telling the Squire to run him out of the Valley."

"He likes you!" Fox protested. "He still tells how easy you done that letter for him at home. Every time I go he asks about you."

"Well, he can ask all he pleases," Chariter said angrily. "If you're a friend to him you better tell him like I say."

She never knew if Fox told Nicodemus or not. If he didn't, he must have told somebody else. Sunday afternoon she heard another knock on the kitchen door and there stood Uncle Nun beaming at her through his brown beard. He had on a clean check shirt and his good black pants he bought across from the market house for dances and funerals.

"How're you doing, girl?" he said heartily.

He came in at her bidding and sat himself down on a painted kitchen chair, leaning it back just far enough to get the front legs off the floor. You could see he knew all the time where he was and couldn't let himself go free like at home.

"Did you hear the news?" he said.

She hadn't and he told her Morg Gandy's house had gone up in smoke across the river. Morg and one of his two young boys had burned up with it. It was that cold night last week. They must have let the stove get red hot. A whole family in West Virginia went the same way the week before. Chariter said she was sorry to hear it. Now wasn't it a pity that little boy had to be taken and not his big mouthed mam?

Uncle Nun wasn't the one to stay on the gloomy side long.

"You think Morg's in heaven now?" he asked genially. "I tell Mam it's a wonder Pap never burned hisself up in his shanty. Now Uncle Robby wouldn't trust himself alone in a house with a fire at night. He'd never come home from the hotel till morning. He told Mam the world was upside down in the night time and he didn't want to fall off."

Chariter almost forgot about Morg Gandy and the two little boys. Uncle Nun went on.

"Did I ever tell you the time Uncle Robby played in the Tinsburg band? He played the drum, knew just when to hit it and when to hold off. They had band practice at the hotel and it was breaking daylight when he come home with his drum. Mam was making breakfast. He told her he'd heard the grandest music on the way. All it lacked, he said, was a bass drum, so he got his off his back and started pounding, bum, bum, bum. Then, he said, the music flew off the telephone wires."

Uncle Nun laughed, looking pleased to get her mind back to normal and cheerful channels. He leaned farther in his chair.

"Licker never hurt anybody. Oh, maybe Uncle Robby had a little too much the time he lost a leg laying on the railroad track, but mostly he could stay on his feet. One time he went to a wake for a fellow from the coal regions they called Mike. I was only a boy and Mam sent me along to see he'd get home. Them miners sat up all night drinking. They gave me some, too. It done me good, made me feel better. About midnight Uncle Robby said wasn't it a shame Mike didn't know the good time they were having. They ought to stand him up so he could see. They done it. Mike fell out the coffin, and I run home like a deer."

Uncle Nun sat there throwing back his head to laugh but the girl noticed him watching her out of one black deilish eye. Oh, she knew why he was giving her all this talk. She had heard the words, running like a deer, before. But if he figured he could make it right for Babe and Fox by telling how he had done the same at their age, he was mistook.

"I have nothing against you, Uncle Nun," she said. "But I do against Nicodemus."

Uncle Nun sobered. He let the front of his chair down.

"You kin let up on him," he said. "I talked to him my own self."

"Well, I hope you made it strong, if he gets mad or not."

"Oh, he didn't get mad," Uncle Nun told her. "He's the best hearted feller. He wouldn't hurt nobody. Besides, he looks up to you. He told me how it was with him and Fox and Babe. He's coming to tell you his own self."

So that was it, the girl thought. Uncle Nun hadn't come to see her after all but to run lackey for the boot-legger. Well, if Nicodemus reckoned he could talk soft to her and still give those two young boys mule, he better watch out.

"He don't need to come and see me, just let off on young ones," she said.

"Now you want to be nice to him," Uncle Nun coaxed. "He's a friend of mine. He done me favors and Pap, too. You ought to see all the business he does. He's no moonshiner. He don't break no revenue laws. He's a hundred percent jobber and wholesaler. He gets it from some big still up in the mountains in Allegheny County. Buys it for cash and brings it down in oil drums in his car. You kin taste the crankcase oil sometimes but it's good for the bowels, they say. Then he bottles it up and puts it on the market. That ain't all he does. He kin get you whatever brand you want. He's a full fledged high class bootlegger, I'm telling you. You don't find him hiding his money in a can under a rock. A can wouldn't hold what he's got. He puts it in the Tinsburg bank."

Chariter didn't say more. If Nicodemus let off on Babe and Fox, she'd forget about him. Then one snowy evening she heard the bang of a tire chain against a fender coming down the lane and the racket of an engine fighting the snow to turn around. After that all was quiet and she reckoned somebody had come to see the squire till she heard the knock on the kitchen door. She opened it and there stood the bootlegger in a sheepskin coat and fur collar grinning at her with a gap in his teeth.

"Nun told me I could come," he said, stamping the snow off his boots.

Well, here he was, the girl told herself, whether she wanted him or not, and if Uncle Nun sent him she better not abuse him too hard. Did he want to come in and take off his hat, she said, for she knew he wouldn't take it off otherwise. In he came like a snowy bear pleased to get in a bee tree.

"I heerd you wanted to see me a while already but never got here," he said.

"Did Uncle Nun tell you what I wanted?" she asked him gravely.

"Oh, he told me," he nodded grinning. "I told Nun, I'd do anything she wanted and maybe she'd write another letter for me? He said I should ask you my self."

"Well, I guess I could," she said. "Have you paper along?"

"It's a business letter," he told her, sobering. "It has to be right. I got it down word for word in my head. All you need do is put it on paper."

He fished makings for the letter from his pocket and she sat down obediently at the kitchen table. He stood behind her straining at the feat of getting ideas out of his head and into her fingers.

"You kin make it out to Paul Pollock," he struggled. "He's a butcher down in Dumont. Now you don't need to put that in. Just tell him I got his order and the goods is ready. Say I got it ready on the day he said but he never showed up. Tell him to stay home Sunday and I'll fetch it down. Tell him to have the money ready. The goods is all made. Tell him not to go away Sunday. I'll put it in a store box. He can count on me. It'll have Condensed Milk on the outside. Now tell him to have the money ready and not go away. Yours truly, Nicodemus. He knows who I am."

She handed him the finished letter. He stood there

149

holding it out in his hand to look at it, a power of satisfaction in his face.

"Now the place where it has to go," he said and fetched a crumpled envelope out of his pocket. She wrote down the address he gave her, folded and enclosed the letter and gave it to him. He took it out.

"You think he'll know to be home Sunday?"

"If he can read," Chariter said.

"Oh, he kin read. He has to write down on paper how much his meat weighs. You better crease it where you had before and put it back. Now I want to pay. How much do I owe you?"

"You don't owe me anything. I'm glad to do it for Uncle Nun."

He looked at her with reproach.

"I'd sooner if you done it for me," he said. "I got plenty money to pay you."

"I wouldn't take money for that from anybody," she told him and picked up his hat for him but he wasn't ready to go.

"I been thinking a long time about you," he said. "I told Nun about it and he said I should come and have a little talk with you. Now maybe you kin guess what about."

"I wouldn't know," she told him.

"Well, I'll say it to you then like I did to Nun," he launched out. "I said, here I am living at the top of the heap, ain't I? He said I was. I said, I got a fine solid going business, don't I? He said I did. I said I got plenty cash in my pocket and more in the bank, isn't that right? He said it was. I said, I got a fine machine to run around with, don't I? He said I did. Now wouldn't a woman be lucky, I said, to get a man like me? He said, by hokey day, she would."

He looked at her proudly. So that's the way the wind blew, she said to herself. Well, let him row his own boat up the stream. He went on.

"I told your Uncle Nun out of this whole valley, who's the best woman for me? He said, what kind of woman did I want? Well, none of these no-good thirsty sluts, I told him. All they want is your money and licker, ain't it so? He said it was. I told him a woman with all this stuff around ought to be temperance. He said nothing else but. She ought to be hefty, I told him, to handle bad customers. He said that wasn't a bad idee. She had to be smart to count money and read a bank book and write a letter when she had to, ain't that right, I said. He said I couldn't be righter. Now what woman out of the valley could match up to that? I asked him. Now maybe you know who she is?"

"Somebody I know?" Chariter asked, unwilling to step in where her name wasn't called.

"Oh, you know her good. She's not old yet but she's full growed."

"Well, it couldn't be me," Chariter said firmly. "Because I'm spoken for."

His face fell.

"I thought you and him fell out?"

"Maybe he fell out with me but I didn't with him."

"It takes only one to bust up," the bootlegger brightened. "They tell me he's got somebody else but don't you tell him I said so. I don't want any trouble with a fire eater like him. I only heerd it some place."

"I won't be seeing him to say anything," she assured him.

He hit her playfully on the shoulder.

"You're no old maid yet, girl," he promised her. "Any time you're ready, just tell old Nicodemus. He'll do anything you say. Any time you say the word."

When he had gone she locked the door and did her evening chores. She told herself she better not go home for a week or two. They'd know all about what went on here tonight. The men especially might figure she'd jumped at the chance. Granpappy would have a hard time getting through his head that she'd turned down a man with a machine, a solid business and cash in the bank. Already he must be counting on getting his mule on tick while others had to have the money in hand. She guessed the news would go farther than the Murdochs. Most of the valley would have heard by tomorrow.

Up in her room she blew out the lamp and undressed

in the dark. Warmth from the kitchen flue came through the wall. Dim light drifted in the window. She could feel the image of trees, sky and snowy fields outside coming in to bathe her arms and haunches, her breasts and cool fundament. She pulled on her bed gown. Oh, she'd sleep alone in her bed tonight but she wouldn't always. No, two men had already come along in her life, and her only sixteen. She could have had either one, had she wanted him as he was. If there were two, there'd be three. The old saying most always came true. Meantime she needed no man to warm up her bed tonight. She could do it her own self.

CHAPTER XIII

Now who would have expected the old saying to fail her and that only two men were to come in her life?

She looked for bad enough when she went home that week. But only the good met her, at first anyway. Uncle Nun beamed at her like they were in some get-rich-quick scheme together and Granpappy for the first time treated her like a grown woman. Oh, they knew she hadn't said yes to Nicodemus right off the reel but neither had she chased him out of the house and fired his coat and hat after. Some things take a little time. Not everybody, Granpappy said, can make up their mind quick like Uncle Robby and Kate Weller who cooked and tended bar at the Red Lion. Uncle Robby popped the question over the bar one night. She stopped drawing beer, took off her apron and they walked two miles to the preacher, her holding him steady on the road.

The preacher wasn't home and till they sat around waiting for him, Uncle Robby got sober and changed his mind. Now Chariter didn't want to wait till her bridesman got sober.

"You done that once before. You don't want to do it again," Uncle Nun said.

Just how did he mean, the girl wondered, and found out soon enough. They told her Fulliam had been home last Sunday when the news about her and Nicodemus went through the valley. He had his Uncle Fulliam's car and looked like a master undertaker in a black overcoat and black undertaker hat. He had picked up Heb along the road and told him he was getting married. It was coming off soon, Heb said. He couldn't remember just when but either this month or next, anyway before the ice went out. They were coming to the valley for the wedding. Heb couldn't remember the name of the woman, if Fulliam ever did tell it, but he called her a good cook and had money coming. Chariter said nothing. Fulliam would have to fetch back a preacher with him as well as a bride, she thought, for it had nobody but the squire in the valley to do lawful marrying.

It was Saturday night after that when she answered the front door bell and found Fulliam Jones standing outside. He had on the fine black undertaker hat and overcoat Heb talked about. Hardly did he give her a look. She might have been a strange hired girl answering the door. The squire came walking out from his office to see who it was.

"Good evening, Squire," the caller said and stepped in the hall without being asked.

"It's Fulliam Jones," Chariter explained, since it was plain from the squire's face that he didn't know him. Then she started to leave.

"I'm getting married, Squire," Fulliam told him. "I came to see if you'd tie the knot."

"Well, I think perhaps we could manage it," the squire said. "When is the happy event to take place?"

"Soon as I can get off a day," Fulliam told him. "We have our house all ready. I'll telephone you before we come."

Chariter was already in the dining room but she couldn't help hearing. Now wasn't he the devil, she told herself, coming up here where she was to get himself married? Oh, that was just like him, figuring how to rub it in on her in front of her folks and the valley. He must still be smarting, she guessed, playing up in front of her this way. It came to her of a sudden she could still get him if she wanted. Oh, she didn't have a scruple against stealing him back from this other woman whoever she was, but she didn't know as she wanted to go against Fate. Granmam always said, never put a sprag in the Wheel of Fortune or try to steer it your own self or the first thing you know it's liable to run you over.

Maybe it was better to let him have this other woman if he wanted her. It might save a lot of dispute and fire eating between them.

"Oh, girl!" she heard Fulliam raise his voice after her. "There's something I want to say to you."

She never turned or came back and he had to follow her to the kitchen.

"Who do you think you're calling at?" she put to him when he showed up at the door. "I'm not your hired girl."

"What's come over you?" he flared back at her. "Daresen't you talk to anybody in the front of the house? Won't he let you out of the kitchen?"

"You never minded being in the kitchen at home," she told him. "Isn't it good enough for you any more?"

"No, and it wouldn't be for you if you were anybody," he came back.

"Maybe you've changed, Fulliam," she said, "but I haven't."

"If you haven't," he told her, "what are you seeing other men for?"

"If you see other women, I can see other men," she said.

"I have to see women on business."

"What business was it took you to Maybel?" she put to him.

"I don't know any Maybel."

"Well, whatever her name is. Or do you know more than one? The squire can't marry you to two or three."

"I only done what I told you I would," he said.

"You told me you were sick of undertaking, too, and going to quit," she reminded him.

"And I would have, too," he declared. "But Uncle Fulliam let me order that machine hearse I wanted. Doors side and back. You can get a coffin in and out either way. It'll run to the cemetery forty miles an hour. No more dogs under every buggy and dog fights in the cemetery. Why, one time I had to get down in the grave and throw out seven dogs before we could let down the coffin. Now I'm getting license, a share in the furniture business and more money, too. Everything's coming around like I figured."

"I'm glad things worked out for you, and all from following your own idea," she told him with a funny set to her mouth.

He threw her a sharp look.

"You could have had part of it if you hadn't been bullheaded."

Now what was he keeping up with this for? she asked herself. He went on, rushing her a little.

"I'm not nobody any more. The whole county knows me now. Last week we had a man on the cooling board. His woman wanted him buried back with her folks. His brothers wanted him buried down with his. We told

158

them the widow had the law on her side to say where to put him. They said we'd never bury him back there. About a thousand people came to see how it turned out. The dead man's brothers laid for us in the cemetery but Uncle Fulliam told the sheriff. He made me a deputy and the pallbearers, too. He gave us pistols to carry and the funeral went off smooth as a greased hog."

"You might have got killed, Fulliam," she said in a low voice.

He looked to see if she was mocking him.

"What would you care?" he said. "Making free with other men. Leading them on to get married."

She let that pass. Let him think it was more than one if he wanted. He went on.

"Is this true or just talk?"

"He asked me," she admitted. "I didn't say I would. Not right off anyway."

"Well, you're doing no fiddling around with me," he said. "Either you go through with it this time or we're through for good."

Now there it was again, she told herself.

"I thought you said you were getting married?"

"I am," he declared. "If not with you, then with somebody else I know."

She looked up at him. He stood there flush faced, reckless, betting everything on this one throw. You'd never reckon it was a marriage bid from the threatening look at her in his eyes. He might soon have undertaking license from the state, but he was still a hothead, full of country vinegar, no telling what he'd do. He needed, she told herself, some solid body like her to hold him down and sober him up so folks could depend on him to bury them right and not go off on a tangent. Oh, he was a devil just the way he done it, but you had to laugh at him inside. He always had to have his way and so sure of getting it he told Heb and the squire before he did her. She stood turning it over in her mind. No use letting him see that she jumped too quick. Easy bought, least valued. She picked up a stove lid with the lifter and started pouring coal.

"Give me that bucket," he said, taking it from her hand, scattering both sides of the fire so that coal fell on the floor. She knew he'd never pick it up. The way he did it showed he expected to stay a while tonight. Otherwise he wouldn't have cared how heavy he banked it. "Well, what do you say?" he asked, giving her a jerk around to see her face.

"I have to talk to the squire first," she said.

"What for? Can't you do what you want your own self?"

"I reckon I could," she told him. "But he has to have somebody look after him here if I go."

"Let him starve," Fulliam said. Now wasn't that like a

man, young and in his prime with a fine undertaker life ahead of him and yet jealous of her poor old harmless squire.

"If I was the kind to run off from him, I could do the same to you," she reminded him.

"You better not," he told her with satisfaction. "You know blamed well what you'd get."

What night was this? Chariter put to herself when Fulliam had gone. Well, she'd be switched if it wasn't Saturday, the same day of the week he had given her the go by and taken off for Maybel. It just went to show that the calendar didn't count as some folks thought. Saturday, they said, was little better than Good Friday, the worst day of the year. That's when they claimed the angels cleaned out the backhouse of heaven, so look out for trouble. You should never start on a journey Saturday, Ant Dib said, and Saturday's child had to work for a living. And now here it was Saturday night with Fulliam back in her life and her going upstairs like she knew all the time he was sure to come around, which she didn't. She had to laugh in bed when she minded how he had gone off half cocked when she said something nice about the squire. You'd hardly reckon men were such jealous creatures. Here he was, young, strong, busting with sap to take over his uncle's trade, and yet lashing out against her poor old granpappy squire, wanting her to run off and leave him alone in this empty pile of a house. Well she guessed men were like that, fractious, greedy, wanting their woman all to themselves even before they were married to her. Oh, she'd give her man all she had and his young ones the same, but never would she let him turn her against her folks.

She thought she better tell the squire at breakfast how things stood so he could start being on the lookout for somebody.

"You reckon you're going to be all right next fall and winter?" was the way she put it to him.

"Why, I hope so Charity." He gave her a sharp glance over his long mustaches.

"Oh, I know I'm not so much that you couldn't get along without me," she told him.

He stopped eating.

"I'm not ungrateful or unappreciative of you, Charity, if that's what you mean."

"You have Mrs. Laird to take care of you. I mean if I had to go away. And maybe I could get Ant Dib to come up. Anyhow there's lots that would jump at the chance to work here."

His dark eyes gazed at her sadly. It always jogged her how those eyes that flashed fierce and fiery on some poor soul at a hearing could look so soft and tender at Miss Belle and lately at her.

"You're planning to leave me, Charity?" he reproached her, and when she told him. "When is this to be?"

"We didn't set the day yet," she told him. "But it won't be right off like he told you."

"You two wouldn't want to stay here with me?" he asked after a little.

"That would be mighty nice," she said. "I could look after you then. I wish we could take you up on it but Fulliam has his undertaking business in Earlville, so I guess we ought to have our house handy."

"I see." He gave her a long slow look and something inside of her felt sad for him. He looked deserted, left out.

"I hope you'll come often and see us when we get to Earlville," she told him. "You're always welcome to a meal or a bed."

"Thank you, Charity," he said. "Is there something I can do for you?"

"You said already you'd marry us," she reminded him. "Down at Granmam's."

He was silent and she thought she spelled out what ran through his mind. He didn't fancy being among the Murdochs in their house in the woods.

"I thought you and your young man might come here," he said. "Most couples do."

"We'd be glad to," she testified, "if we didn't ought to have a wedding our folks could come to."

"You could still come here," he said gravely. "We have plenty of room and I should be able to provide that much for you."

She stood struck of a heap. This was something only Fulliam would have the gall to think of, a wedding in the squire's big house, even if he might be her granpappy. She felt she had to warn him how many folks there might be. She started naming family, neighbors and friends. Every time she guessed that was all, another name popped into her mind. Till it was over she reckoned the squire would surely back down but only once did he draw his breath twice. That was when she named Granpap Murdoch.

"You mean Hercules Murdoch who was up before me for arson last summer?" he asked, and when she nodded, "Well, I hope he'll be on better behavior here."

"Oh, he wouldn't dare do anything at your place," she said. "He might as well do it to me. He claims he never did it to those barns anyhow. He says some who don't like him made it up against him."

He gave her a look.

"I've found your judgement pretty sound, Charity," he told her. "I hope your affections haven't run away with it now."

CHAPTER XIV

THE Murdochs heard her invitation to the squire's coldly. You'd reckon from their faces this was to be a hanging instead of a wedding. She knew well enough what was the matter, nothing with Fulliam and nothing with her. No, she had guessed how it would be before she told them. That's why she had put it nice and hurtless as she could.

Her mother came out with it.

"Isn't our house good enough for you?" she said.

"You can't put that on me!" the girl answered her quick. "Fulliam asked him to tie the knot and that's where he does it. We can't expect him to come down here. Besides, he wants you up there. We spoke your names, especially you, Mam and Granpappy."

"Well, he don't need look for me," Granpap bristled.

"Or me either," her mother told her.

"I'd hate to be married without my own mam at my wedding," Chariter said.

"What does Fulliam say?" Granmam asked.

"I don't care what Fulliam says," her mam said.

Oh, they wouldn't give in easy, the girl knew. She didn't know as she blamed them. She had to admit it looked like she held herself above them. But give her time, she'd break them down. They couldn't hold out on her forever. She'd just wait till their pride stopped smarting. The worst, she guessed, would be holding Fulliam off till they came around.

That's what she thought and it gave her a turn when he fell in so quick. Now what went on in his mind, she asked herself, that he jumped at the chance of putting off his wedding?

"April'll be here before we know it," she had promised him.

"How about June?" he went her one better. "That's the time for roses. Most women like to get married in June."

She felt taken aback. It wasn't like Fulliam. Never did he want to put off anything. Once for it, nothing could wait. It had to come off right now. Tomorrow was too late. And now some time nearly a half a year off was the very daddle for him. Had he made the bargain with her too quick and was he trying to wriggle out?

Well, if that was his notion, he was free as a bird to fly off, she told herself. But never would she make it easy for him. Meantime she had her hands full with her family. The first she worked on were Granmam and Ant Dib. They still set their faces against her but every time she went home they gave in a little. Uncle Nun stood her off longer. He said he might come if his friend, Nicodemus, was invited. Mam gave her a hard rough tumble. You could tell the way she bit off her words that it still ate her to go up there. In time she guessed she could make it but Chariter wouldn't take any guessing. She had to count on her, she said. More than anybody else save perhaps Fulliam. At the end her mam still sulled but was willing. Granpappy was the hardest to win over. He cursed he'd never darken the door of that shyster squire. He fought her tooth and nail before she got the hate out of him. She could almost feel her little girl love back for him when she swore with her hand held over his rebellious thumping heart that he'd come.

Once Granpap gave up the fort, Nobe came around and Tom said it was no time to hold a grudge at a wedding. And now she knew all was well when Uncle Nun started baiting her with stories.

"Don't he write you love letters?" he wanted to know. "If he does, you don't want to do like Barnaby

Hill when that woman wrote him one. He had the school teacher read it to him with his hands over her ears so she wouldn't hear what it said."

Oh, every time Chariter came home now, he had a new story for her, like the long one about Sam Giller who drank too much and wouldn't go to bed on his wedding night. No, he said his bed would have to come to him, and when he woke up sober he was sleeping with his pappy in law who had a hook for a hand.

Now wouldn't it be something, the girl told herself, that if after the whole family had sweetened on her, Fulliam would go sour? Late in May he put off the day from June first to the fifteenth and then to the twenty ninth. She half looked for him to put it off again, but this time she made up her mind. Either they'd be married at six o'clock Saturday the twenty ninth or it was off for good. She wouldn't let Fulliam make a fool of her and all her folks, even if he had just buried an Earlville man in a thousand dollar copper coffin.

On the big day everybody showed up but him and Granpappy. Granmam and Ant Dib came early to help Mrs. Laird get the wedding rations ready. Ed Fridely and his woman came to the back door as did Jack Peeples. his wife and Vince Foote, while the Joneses came to the front. Most showed up on foot except Fulliam's uncle and ant from Earlville who rode in their machine, Mrs. Stevens in hers and the bootlegger in his, grinning from ear to ear and beckoning men and boys to the back seat where he had liquid refreshment suitable to the occasion.

"Where's Fulliam?" they kept putting up to the bride.

"I don't know any more than you," she told them.

She was all ready in her white and "yaller" bride's dress. Granmam had bought the goods for her across from the market house. Ant Dib had helped her cut it out and sew it up. The two clocks in the parlor struck six times and still no Fulliam.

"Now you know how it feels," her mam told her darkly.

But Chariter wouldn't fret yet. If his uncle and ant were here and his pap, too, he better come if he knew what was good for him. Sure enough not long after a car sounded in the lane. They looked out. There was Fulliam in his good suit climbing down from a fine big black machine. It looked shiny and new through the red valley dust that faintly coated it.

"Well, he got here, so he did," Ed Pridely said.

"It's our new hearse sedan," Uncle Fulliam told them, swelling a little with pride.

Now wasn't that just like Fulliam and his uncle, the girl thought, having him come in a new machine hearse to advertise their business in the valley and show how up to date they were? The men had to go out to look it over. Chariter could hear Fulliam telling its good points, how the glass doors let a body in and let it out, how much it weighed and cost, how long they had to wait for it, how it had to go to the shop when they did get it and came back for good only today.

Chariter didn't mind the hearse. To meet a funeral was good luck, they said, and that went for a hearse, too. But to put off a wedding was a sign she didn't know as she liked. She hoped all it meant today was that the rest of her life her man would come home late for dinner and bed. She didn't need any hearse to tell her that. She knew what Fulliam was when she went into this and long before. Good or bad she would have to take him as he was, formaldehyde and all. She'd get used to that smell like a farmer's town-body wife had to get used to the smell of manure.

The best part, she told herself, was that Fulliam showed up feeling so high at his wedding, even though it did come from a hearse. If that new machine of his could put pleasure in his sober work, she was for it. Now folks were moving up the big front parlor. You could see they weren't easy and free like they would have been at Granmam's. But where was Granpap? The squire tramped in from the office with the little book in his hand. It grew quiet then. He worked his way up and stood with his back to the window. She and Fulliam had to stand in front of him. A little chill ran over Chariter at the sound of his deep lawful voice.

"We are gathered here in the face of this company to join together this man and this woman as is honorable among all men and therefore not to be entered into lightly."

Chariter half closed her eyes so she could taste the solemn words. Standing there it flew in her head, what if the squire would take it on himself to say her real name? When he came to, "Do you take this woman as your lawful wife?" what if instead of Chariter Murdoch, he said Chariter Goddem? No, he better not say that if he wanted to keep peace with Tom Leck, Nobe Gandy and the Murdochs. He would never say it in a hundred years anyhow. It was just the flighty notion of a bride on tenterhooks, something she knew she never should have thought of when the Lord had already given her all he had. But why did He have to punish her so quick for it? she asked herself, and such a dressing down as came to her now? Ever since she could remember she had hated one called-out word above all others. It seldom failed to fetch to her mind the smell of burned horses and cattle laying around on the black ground and to her heart the ugly thing folks said, that her own granpap was at the bottom of it.

She couldn't believe it when she heard that word, Fire!, called out today.

"Squire!" right afterward Harrison Laird's hoarse voice bawled at the front door.

The squire still stood there unwilling to lay down his book though others pushed for the outside. Not easy would she forget the cruel look he gave her. Oh, she knew what went through his head as plain as what had gone through her own. She guessed she had been a fool. The rest of her flesh and blood had meant it when they said they'd come to her wedding. For her sake they had let up in their spite long enough to show their faces. But not him. All this time he must have been scheming over how to get back at the squire and at her too. She knew now why when he swore he'd come, his heart under her hand had thumped so obstreperously.

Pretty soon, hardly a soul was left in the house. When Chariter got outside Uncle Nun had made himself fire boss, bawling out what they should do, throw out burning hay and straw with pitchforks, run buckets from the watering trough. Lucky the cows were in the field, but the horses and old Jacko, the Holstein bull, had to be pulled and beaten to safe ground. Most was thick "yaller" smoke now. Till it was over Uncle Nun's best green checked shirt and Uncle Heb's red one had turned black with sweat and charcoal. The rest of the men might have been blackamoors. The barn looked sick with a gaping dark hole in its fine painted white side.

"You're lucky, Squire, you had a fire crew all ready at your house," Vince Foote told him cheerfully but you could see the squire didn't hold to that. No, he had no notion he was lucky. His long tailed coat looked a sight, his eyes bloodshot, his mouth set behind his mustaches. Most gave him a wide berth. If this was still going to be a wedding, Chariter thought, you wouldn't know it. Ant Dib's face looked long as Uncle Heb's winter underwear hanging on the line. Her own face felt not much shorter.

"It must a been them boys smoking in the cow stable entry," Uncle Nun tried to cheer her.

"It must a been," she said but her words sounded empty. "When did you see him?"

"Who?" Uncle Nun said, "Oh him? I ain't seen him since yesterday. Now don't you let this get you down, girl. You couldn't help it."

Maybe she could and maybe she couldn't, the girl told herself. No matter how forehanded you tried to be, bad luck could always get around it and bamfoozle you at the end. All these weeks she had listened to Granpappy's promises, swallowed his fair words, let herself be deceived by his guile. Why, she had even got back some of her old time feeling for him since this was the day she'd have to take leave of them all. And while she played the fool, he had been setting on his grudge a hatching it out.

"When did you see him?" she put to Granmam but Granmam said she hadn't and neither had Ant Dib. All the time her mam stood by with a bitter face.

"They won't tell you," she called out. "They don't want to disgrace you on your wedding day. They told me I darsen't say nothing either. But if you ask me, I'll tell you. Your granpap ain't here because he's in Dumont in jail."

"In jail!" Chariter said. "Since when?"

"Since yesterday."

"Oh, Mam, isn't that wonderful!" the girl cried, throwing her arms around her. "And all this time he's been innocent as a poor lamb."

Her mam looked startled.

"You mean that dirty old he-goat!" she said angrily. "We had so much to do getting ready for this we was fool enough to send him to Dumont for your present. We'd picked it out at Kellers across from the market house. Sam Nickerson gave him a ride in. All he had to do was pay for it and bring it home. But the old fool spent the money getting drunk. Then he got in a couple of fights and Aderman McKenna had him locked up."

Chariter thought she had never heard sweeter words. She ran to the squire, telling him the news.

"Can't we do something to get him out?" she begged. "I don't want folks saying he was in jail on my wedding day."

The squire's face was a caution. She couldn't spell out if he felt better or worse, if he believed it or doubted.

"I'll talk to McKenna," he said and stood up by his

telephone to call the alderman. Oh, Chariter could tell by listening that they knew each other and that all this time Granpappy was safe and sound behind prison walls. The squire didn't hem or haw. "Could I pay his fine and get him out, Alderman?" he asked in that deep voice like he meant business. "I'll send you a check. Wait a minute. Can you get him out tonight and send him here in a cab? It's for a special occasion. I'll pay the driver."

Chariter hugged the squire. He looked mighty funny for a minute, like he didn't fancy such things with valley folks looking on. The girl didn't care. For half a cent she'd have done more. A juicy kiss from a young girl might do his rusty old vitals some good. Now wasn't it a wonder, she told herself, how quick your luck could change? It must be the back luck from the put-off wedding running out and good luck from the hearse coming in. All had been gloom and vinegar before. Now the sun was pushing out sweetening the world, and that sun was Granpappy. He wasn't here yet but he was coming. She stood up for the second time for her vows, more beholden to life and living than the first. The words from the book sounded like they had been set down just for her and Fulliam. Her heart swelled at the thought of all her folks closing ranks here around her. They had come to see her and Fulliam yoked together. Granpappy would miss that, though he could still see her in her bride's dress. But wasn't it crazy of her choking up once it was all over? Here she was fresh married and making a fool of herself right off the reel.

Fulliam scowled at her.

"Well, I don't know as I ever saw you do that before," he told her.

"And you might never again," she said back to him, adding quickly against fate, "Unless we have bad luck with a young one."

Uncle Nun came pushing up with his brown beard jovial.

"How come you know you're going to have any?" he rallied her. "I mind we had a dry heifer once. She never did come in fresh. We had to sell her to the butcher."

"You needn't fret about a Murdoch," Granmam settled him. "That's the trouble. They bear right off. She'll give Fulliam more'n he kin feed."

"We'll feed them all right," Fulliam told her.

Her mother and Ant Dib made tracks for the kitchen and Granmam soon after. The ham and chicken and other rations had been held over mighty long, but they'd have to do. Most ate in the kitchen and Ant Dib tried to get Granpappy out there when he came. Granmam complained loudly how unwashed and unshaven he was, and his shirt filthy. He would have nothing of them. He was his own man now. Hadn't he got the best of his enemies, walked out of jail free as a bird, ridden all the way out here in a pay taxicab bragging to the driver how his granddaughter was getting married at the squire's? And you think now he'd eat in the kitchen? Not him. His place was in the dining room sitting down with the bride and bridesman, Tom Leck and Nobe Gandy, the squire and the Joneses at the long walnut table. Once there he wouldn't eat. He claimed he wasn't hungry, only thirsty. What he wanted was to give his new grandson advice from a long married man.

"Now you want to watch out you don't bury anybody alive!" he warned sagely. "I mind yet when Hildy Weaver died. She'd told Clem Miller she wanted her old parrot buried with her. Clem had to knock down half the stuff in the house till he caught that bird. Then he give it chloroform and put it in with the old lady. They was just letting down the coffin when a voice come out of the grave. 'Maw! Oh, Maw!' it said. I heerd it myself. The preacher heerd it, too. Clem said it was nothing but that damned parrot but lots of folks said it sounded like Hildy. It hurt Clem's business so he had to sell out and go to Cumberland where they didn't know nothing about Hildy Weaver."

"Don't worry about us, Granpap," Fulliam told him. "Just look out they don't put you in a box some time when you're pickled."

"I'm afeard of no box," Granpap came back at him stoutly. "I'm like my cousin Jake in Porter Valley. He kep his box underneath his bed for thirty years. Quartered oak with silver handles. He got it cheaper buying two when his woman died. Every so often he used to pull it out and lay down in it to see how it felt to be dead and buried. He tried to get the preacher to preach with him laying in it so he could hear his own funeral sermon, but the preacher wouldn't."

"Well, Uncle Fulliam and I know somebody who would," Fulliam said. "That long winded fellow out at the Long Run Church. Last month we had two funerals the same Saturday afternoon. We set one up in his church for two o'clock and said we'd be back from the other one at three thirty to do the burying. We told him to keep preaching till we got there. But we couldn't make it. When we got back at five he was still going strong. We had a time shutting him off to bury by daylight."

Granpappy made a face. He didn't like a new grandson telling him stories. He was the story teller.

"Well, you better not pull any of your undertaker tricks on me," he charged. "And don't pretty me up either. I never forgot what they done to poor old George Carter. The undertaker from Freeburg talked his folks into letting him take him. He claimed if he didn't work on him right off, rigor mortis would start eating him up. Well, he brought him back next day and was so tickled over what he done he put an electric light from a battery over his face. The Carter boys took one look. 'That ain't Paw!' they hollered. 'What you done with Paw?' If the undertaker hadn't lit out of there, he might have got shot and would have served him right too. Why, he'd shaved poor old George, cut his hair and put a fancy white collar and tie on him. Nobody'd ever seen him like that. He didn't look like hisself at all. Nobody's going to spoil me like that when my time comes."

"You won't be here to know it, Granpap," Fulliam said cheerfully.

"I won't!" Granpap looked mad. "Where will I be?"

"You'll be in heaven plucking a harp."

Most everybody had to laugh at the idea of Culy Murdoch in heaven with a harp. Fulliam jumped up.

"Now me and Chariter have to go," he said. "We might have a call at Earlville and never know it."

Chariter rather would have stayed at her own wedding a while longer. But she reckoned she better not start leading her man around by the nose the first night. She knew before she married him that Fulliam liked to be on the go. All these people she had seen before and would again some time, God willing. Besides, it was getting late and she felt curious about that house in Earlville Fulliam said he had got ready for her.

Her bridesman carried out her traps and stowed them behind the glass of the hearse. He closed the doors, boosted her up to the seat and started cranking. It took a world of clickings, then the engine came to life. It would be a noisy thing to live with, the girl thought. Thank heaven Fulliam didn't mind. He shinned up beside her and blew his horn for room. He hadn't thought to turn around when he first came. Now he had to work that long hearse back and forwards in front of all. He came close to hitting the fence coming around before he got free. Then Chariter bent out to look back and wave.

Well, here she was, she told herself as they went down the valley past the home lane and every house and place she knew, here she was going off in the hearse happier than she'd ever been before, with a new life in front of her and sad only for them she had to leave behind.

CONRAD RICHTER was born in Pennsylvania, the son, grandson, nephew, and great-nephew of clergymen. He was intended for the ministry, but at thirteen he declined a scholarship and left preparatory school for high school, from which he was graduated at fifteen. After graduation he went to work. His family on his mother's side was identified with the early American scene, and from boyhood on he was saturated with tales and the color of Eastern pioneer days. In 1928 he and his small family moved to New Mexico, where his heart and mind were soon captured by the Southwest. From this time on he devoted himself to fiction. *The Sea of Grass* and *The Trees* were awarded the gold medal of the Societies of Libraries of New York University in 1942. *The Town* received the Pulitzer Prize in 1951, and *The Waters of Kronos* won the 1960 National Book Award for fiction. His other novels include *The Fields* (1946), *The Light in the Forest* (1953), and *The Lady* (1957).

A NOTE ON THE TYPE

THE TEXT of this book was set on the Linotype in *Janson*, a recutting made direct from type cast from matrices long thought to have been made by the Dutchman Anton Janson, who was a practicing type founder in Leipzig during the years 1668–87. However, it has been conclusively demonstrated that these types are actually the work of Nicholas Kis (1650–1702), a Hungarian, who most probably learned his trade from the master Dutch type founder Dirk Voskens. The type is an excellent example of the influential and sturdy Dutch types that prevailed in England up to the time William Caslon developed his own incomparable designs from these Dutch faces.

Composed, printed, and bound by
The Haddon Craftsmen, Inc., Scranton, Pa.
Typography and binding design based on
originals by W. A. Dwiggins